IF THIS BE TREASON

Benedict Arnold and George Washington's Spies

J. Kenneth Metz

Copyright © 2017 J. Kenneth Metz.
Publisher Address: 285 East Main Street—Frostburg, MD 21532
Publisher Phone Number: 301-689-3713
Legal Name: James Kenneth Metz

This book is a work of fiction. Any references to historical figures, nations, governments, locations, and events are meant only to simulate history, not to represent actual history.

Dialogue by historical characters and fictional characters is fictitious and should not be considered real. The only exceptions involve speeches by the Benedict Arnold character, by the John André character, and by the George Washington character (as noted in appendix A).

ISBN: 978-0-9883901-1-9 (sc)
ISBN: 978-0-9883901-2-6 (e)

Library of Congress Control Number: 2017910796

Lulu Publishing Services rev. date: 07/21/2017

To my grandchildren and my great-grandchildren: Kade Kahl, Kacey (Kahl) Stafford, Meshach Metz, Peyton Kahl, Megan Metz, Elijah Metz, Masek Metz, "Jo Jo" Stafford, and Blake Stafford. May they never forget their Pop.

ACKNOWLEDGMENTS

The author is indebted to his son, Russell, for his diligent proofreading of the manuscript and to his wife, Julia, and his grandson, Kade, for their assistance with the prologue and the dust jacket.

PROLOGUE

*The treason of which I stand convicted loses all its guilt, has
been sanctified as a duty, and will be ennobled as a sacrifice.*
—Thomas Francis Meagher

In 1765, Patrick Henry, member of the Virginia House of Burgesses, was speaking to his fellow legislators in protest of British King George III's oppressive Stamp Act. In his speech, Mr. Henry was attempting to draw a comparison between one historical traitor and another: "Caesar had his Brutus; Charles the First his Cromwell; and George the Third—"

At the mere mention of King George's name in the delegate's roll call of traitors, Henry's speech was abruptly interrupted by one or more Tory legislators (loyal to the Crown), who cried out, "Treason! Treason!" Henry immediately replied to his audience with his now famous rejoinder: "If this be treason, make the most of it!"

If This Be Treason echoes Patrick Henry's answer to the scolding by his Tory critics. Much of the book is dedicated to the proposition that one man's traitor could well be another man's patriot.

That 1765 Henry-Tory encounter is illustrative of the late eighteenth-century state of tensions between America's patriots and Americans still loyal to King George. Tory colonists saw themselves as the Loyalists and saw the upstart Americans as traitors. The soon-to-be revolutionaries, of course, held the diametrically opposite viewpoint.

In the War for Independence (1775–1781), American general Benedict Arnold was one such patriot turned traitor, according to American history books. According to British texts, Arnold's defection and plan to turn over an American fort to the British merely marked the return of a reformed rebel to the bosom of his ancestral motherland.

In 1780, Arnold schemed to sell out America's fort at West Point to his British brethren. Benedict's coconspirators in the West Point plot were Benedict's wife, Peggy, and Peggy's romantic interest, British colonel John André.

During the Revolutionary War, in contrast to Colonial patriots who were writing of their mutual pledge to each other of their lives, their fortunes, and their sacred honor, the male Arnold was writing passes for British colonel André to get him through American lines, and the female Arnold was sending encrypted messages to André—all the while treasuring a lock of his hair, which she had secretly hidden from her husband.

The status of the Benedict-Peggy-John triangle ebbed and flowed during the course of the long American War for Independence until General George Washington's secret citizen-spy network, the Culper Ring, uncovered the threesome's West Point conspiracy.

Washington's subsequent foiling of the Arnold-Arnold-André West Point scheme put the trio of conspirators out of commission and left the fate of Peggy and her two men trembling in the balance.

One question worth asking is whether the Americans or the British saw Peggy Arnold—because of her role in the West Point plot—as any more or less beautiful than before, considering that beauty is in the eye of the beholder.

Another question is if Benedict Arnold actually *betrayed* a country (his new, emergent America) or if he, in effect, *served* a country (his ancestral English homeland), granting that, like beauty, treason is in the eye of the beholder.

CHAPTER 1
Philadelphia, 1777

In 1777, America's major Benedict Arnold is a hero. During the War of American Independence, Arnold has become famous for his victories over the British at Fort Ticonderoga and Bemis Heights. But being a hero and being famous have not made Benedict Arnold happy.

Arnold is unhappy because the death of his wife, Margaret Mansfield Arnold, in 1775, left Benedict to rear their three children alone. Benedict is no mother; it is common knowledge that he is hardly a father. Having immersed himself in his all-consuming military career, Arnold had early on forfeited all parenting rights and responsibilities to Margaret.

Unfortunately, his heroics on the battlefield have gained Arnold neither the quality nor the quantity of notoriety that he has sought—his superior officers having stolen the acclaim, he contends. For months, Arnold has not been paid any wages by his government for his services rendered. He lives from hand to mouth. Poverty has exacerbated Benedict Arnold's unhappiness.

And as recently as September 26 of this year, 1777, Arnold has been observed openly weeping at word of the British army's capture of Philadelphia. Benedict Arnold cannot fathom that his beloved, fledgling nation's capital city has fallen into the hands of the enemy. Demoralization has compounded Benedict Arnold's unhappiness.

Meanwhile, in Philadelphia, and in contrast to Arnold's condition, a British colonel, John André, is basking in the limelight. Residing now in what once was the domicile of America's venerable Benjamin Franklin, the

1

wealthy André has risen from lieutenant to the rank of colonel at a young age. The handsome British officer is also a poet, an artist, and the life of Philadelphia parties.

During this American Revolution, approximately one-third of America's population sides with the rebels, about one-third remains loyal to the Crown, but another one-third is neutral, awaiting the war's outcome in order to decide whose side they shall be on. One of those fence-sitters is Judge Edward Shippen IV, a rich, politically connected, prominent figure in Pennsylvania.

Bending with the winds of political events, Judge Shippen could just as well be a patriot's patriot or a Loyalist's Loyalist. Currently, Shippen's weather vane favors the easterly breeze of the battle-victorious redcoats. The judge is more than cordial to Philadelphia's new British landlords, opening his home to prominent local Loyalists as well as to King George's officials and British army officers.

Today, a sunny late-autumn day in 1777, Shippen has graciously invited John André to his fashionable South Fourth Street mansion. Ostensibly, Shippen has asked Colonel André there to make sketches of Shippen's youngest daughter, Peggy, all on Judge Shippen's nickel, of course.

But beneath Shippen's patronizing-of-the-arts smoke screen is a clandestine matchmaking. Edward Shippen hopes to make a marital match between his Peggy and the handsome, wealthy André.

Shippen personally receives Colonel André at the mansion's front door and is now leading the young redcoat through the Shippen household to Peggy Shippen's bedroom, where a maid, Laura, is attending to the young lady, who is seated at her bed's edge.

As the two men enter the room, Judge Shippen says, "Colonel André, I wish to introduce you to my daughter, Peggy. Peggy, this is Colonel John André of his Majesty's Royal Army. He has graciously consented to steal himself away from the manifold duties of his office so as to kindly do your portrait today."

Peggy looks up, rises, and quickly studies the tall, handsome young man who has entered her boudoir. After sizing up his broad shoulders and tight leggings, she curtsies. "Good day, Colonel André."

André is doing his own studying, immediately aware of the pretty young girl's fine hair, fine skin, and fine figure. He bows. "My pleasure, my young lady."

Judge Shippen continues, "Laura, you may come with me." He turns to exit.

Peggy politely offers a mild protest, saying, "But, Father, you are leaving us unattended?"

"Of course," answers the judge. "John André is a gentleman … as you will discover."

Peggy's father and maid exit, and the judge closes the bedroom door behind him.

John André nods toward a nearby furniture piece. "May I deposit my art satchel on this chair, Miss Shippen?"

"Certainly," answers the golden-haired beauty, "but, Colonel, please call me Peggy. You need not be so formal, what with my father now having left us … and having left us behind closed doors and all." She smiles. "And what is it that you wish first for me to do?"

"The light, Miss Peggy. I fear that none of the chairs in this room is sufficiently illuminated for me to do justice to your countenance."

"My what?"

"I mean that a better light, a brighter light, Miss Shippen, should permit my eyes—or any other artist's eyes, for that matter—to drink in the beauty of your complexion, the energy in your eyes, the intoxication in your smile."

She is silent. For the first time in her life, the seventeen-year-old Peggy is hearing a man, particularly such a charming and handsome young man, speaking such flattery about her appearance. She is dazzled. She hears his words and repeats them to herself: *Beauty of my complexion, energy in my eyes, intoxication in my smile. Oh my!*

She is beyond fascinated with this man—to the extent that she is only able to manage, barely above a whisper, "Intoxicating?"

"Intoxicating to the very soul of me, sweet lady."

She thinks, *Is this prince for real, or am I still abed?*

John André says, "Might I not move a chair for me and a chair for you nearer to the window's light?"

She manages a faint "Certainly" accompanied by an involuntary, broad smile.

As he lifts two heavy chairs to the illuminated section of the room, Peggy mildly gasps. *It takes both me and Laura together to heft just one of those chairs even a few inches. This prince is as strong as he is charming.*

André gestures to the chair nearer to the window.

Peggy sits herself and asks, "How should I pose?"

André says, "Well, it is the bust type of portrait that your family wishes to evolve from your sitting. Do you have any wardrobe that would enhance the parts of you—that is, the parts of you from the waist up?"

Peggy thinks, *Well, this man might be the officer, but he just might not be an officer and a gentleman.* She hesitates to answer, admiring André's uniform and the filling of it by his musculature. *And I think I shall be quite happy if this officer proves to be no gentleman at all.*

"I have just the idea," she finally announces. "Will you excuse me as I make a slight alteration to this attire?" She strokes her blouse sleeves.

He nods, acknowledging her intentions.

"Will you hand me my scissors?" She points.

He lifts the scissors from a small, nearby table and hands them to her.

She adds, "Will you now turn your back?"

He obliges, and with a fixity of purpose, she puts the scissors to her blouse's high neck collar, cutting down at an angle in two swipes to remove from the blouse a large "V"-shaped area of material from the neck downward. She sits and says, "Will this do?"

John André turns. It is now his turn not to speak. Peggy's cutting has revealed a goodly portion of her youthful and ample bosom. André is unaccustomed to any female behavior such as this, either on the east side or on the west side of the Atlantic. His artist's eyes are fixed, and he is enthralled. Eventually he replies, "Will your family approve?"

"You may study as little of me as you wish or as much of me as you wish, John André. You may sketch as little of me as you wish or as much of me as you wish," she purrs, almost singing. "We need not bother my parents with whatever procedures you require in your artistic endeavor." *If he wants a bust, I shall give him a bust.*

"But you have ruined your blouse just for me to sketch you."

"And I would gladly ruin more of my dress for you, Colonel, even ruin my reputation just for you, sir."

A blush blossoms on the Colonel's cheeks. "Whatever do you mean?"

She nods toward her bed. "I'll show you what I mean. Take me to my bed … and take me."

John André abruptly turns on his heel. "I fear that I can stay no more here with you, Miss Shippen. I must inform your father of your behavior."

"Kind sir, do you not like my countenance? Do you not like my bust?"

"Of course, of course. You perchance, young lady, just might be the most perfect work of art that these eyes have ever beheld, but that is not the issue. My work is as an officer of the king. It matters not my desire for something in this room. What matters is my desire to fulfill my duty as representative of the Crown."

"Then there is something in this room that you desire, that you would desire having?"

"Of course, of course!" André abruptly lifts his hands to his face, shielding his eyes from the voluptuous temptress before him. "Do not ask me such," he requests in an almost panting breath.

Peggy, sensing the obvious weakening in the resolve by her prey, issues a self-congratulatory smile. *This will be my first romantic conquest,* she thinks, her own breath and pulse accelerating.

André's eye-hiding interlude ends as he lowers his hands from his face and explains, "But you must see, Miss Peggy, you are placing me in a very awkward situation. Your parents are too near, you are too young, and I am too attentive to sense of duty."

"But I plead with you to be more attentive to me, Johnny."

Hearing this sweet lass address him so informally evokes in André a smile, which he immediately decides to quit, lest the lady see and gain undue encouragement from his visceral reaction to her calling him *Johnny*. André says, "Perhaps, perhaps under other circumstances, perhaps when you are older."

Not discouraged in the least, Peggy says. "Next week, I shall be a week older. You will come to me then, won't you, Johnny?"

André, this time being able to ignore her calling him "Johnny," resists, "No, Miss Shippen, no!"

"Next month I shall be a month older."

"No, again, young lady, no!"

"Next year I shall be a year older."

He does not answer.

André's hesitation prompts her to add, "Pray, do not tell my father. Come back to this bedroom in one year. I shall await you. Please don't tell."

After considering and reconsidering, André says, "A year ... I shall give you a year to change your mind. And I shall not tell."

"I can't wait for 1778, Johnny. Can you?"

His eyes focused on the table holding his art supplies, the colonel appears not to have even heard Peggy's last remark. He does not reply; instead, he walks to the table, gathers his satchel, bids Miss Shippen adieu, and exits.

Peggy Shippen has discovered—much to her regret—that the present Colonel André indeed is a gentleman, but the possibility of his returning to her bed in the months ahead gives Peggy hope that the future Colonel André will by then have forgotten how to behave so gentlemanly.

CHAPTER 2
The Culper Spy Ring

Flashback to 1776. Early in the Revolutionary War, the commander in chief of the Continental Army, General George Washington, had become aware of the dearth of good intelligence regarding the Crown's troop numbers and their movements. Subsequently, on September 10, 1776, one of Washington's captains, Nathan Hale of Connecticut, becomes the United States' first spy when he volunteers for a mission to spy upon the British behind enemy lines in New York City.

Nathan Hale also becomes America's first spy to die. In New York, the Brits soon recognize Hale to be a patriot, discover incriminating notes on his person, arrest him, and hang him.

After that failed espionage mission by Hale, Washington knows what he really needs is actual New Yorkers, that is, inconspicuous persons in place in the city who can pass as Loyalists. Consequently, in May 1778, General Washington chooses Major Benjamin Tallmadge to create such a spy network of New Yorkers.

Because Benjamin Tallmadge had been a classmate and roommate of Nathan Hale at Yale College, Tallmadge is eager to take up where Captain Hale had left off. Having been born on Long Island, Tallmadge has ties to his local community from where he recruits Abraham Woodhull and Robert Townsen to become resident spies.

The major takes the code number 721 and the code name John Bolton. General George Washington gives Abraham Woodhull (Agent 722) the code name Samuel Culper (a play on the county name, Culpeper, in General Washington's native Virginia).

Townsen becomes Agent 723, or Samuel Culper Jr. (the alias chosen because Benjamin Tallmadge actually has a younger brother named Samuel). With so many Culper aliases in the espionage network, the spies come to call themselves the Culper Ring.

Also in June of '78, all British military personnel are ordered to vacate Philadelphia. King George fears that in Philadelphia his army would be sitting ducks for the navy of France—which has recently joined the Americans in the war against him—whose fleet is now nearing North America. Therefore, by June 18, all of the Crown's troops have left Philadelphia, most of them being transferred to New York City.

Of course, this means that British colonel John André now is nowhere near the Edward Shippen mansion, nowhere near the judge's (soon-to-be eighteen-year-old) eager and willing daughter, and in no way able to keep his almost-year-old planned rendezvous with her.

And the tide is turning for the politics of Edward Shippen. The Brits have been swept from the City of Brotherly Love, and a rebel government has flowed in. Shippen will kiss the hands of Philadelphia's new landlords and sweeten the kisses with honey if need be.

Continental Army commander-in-chief Washington needs a military governor in Philadelphia, and he chooses the popular Major Benedict Arnold for that duty. On June 19, Major Arnold moves into the Penn house, the military headquarters previously occupied by Great Britain's general Howe prior to the British withdrawal from Philadelphia to New York City.

It does not take long for the pragmatist's pragmatist, Edward Shippen, to begin to open his townhouse on Society Hill to parties and balls for Philadelphia's new masters, including Colonial bigwigs, city dignitaries, and Continental Army officers, including the new commander of the town, Major Benedict Arnold.

Two weeks before one of his renowned dinner/dances, Judge Shippen knocks at his daughter's door. Peggy calls out her usual, "Entrez, sil vous plait."

Holding a small envelope, which he is opening, Edward Shippen enters, waving the envelope's contents for Peggy to see. "He's coming to dine and dance a fortnight from today," he exclaims.

"Colonel John André?"

"No, no, no. Not Colonel André. He is now the enemy. 'Tis a more important officer coming, this city's very own military governor, himself, Major Benedict Arnold."

Peggy waves back at him her own piece of paper. "I'm not interested, Father, but I am interested in this note, just arrived this morning. It comes from my Johnny André in New York. He misses us, Father. He misses you and Mom. But mostly me! Can we visit him?"

"Out of the question, lass! New York if off limits! It is in enemy hands now.

"Enemy hands?"

"You see, the Brits used to be our friends, but they are now the enemy. By all means, this André chap is off limits for you ... a note from André, you say? How do you come by it?"

"Some man I had not seen before ... he was in some hurry."

"Let me see it."

She hands the judge the paper.

Edward unfolds it, peers at its script, and says, "This is gibberish! It is all numbers, no words. Is the man an intellectual backslider?"

"In no way, Father. It is in code. He and I have corresponded for months using encrypted messages. In his letters, Johnny has taught me how to do it. Johnny is the spy master for General Henry Clinton, you know."

"No, I do not know, nor do I care. And did I twice hear you refer to him as *Johnny*?"

"I call him Johnny, and I love my Johnny. May he visit us, Father?"

"Love your Johnny? Don't be daft, girl! André to visit here at Society Hill? Don't be dafter! He'd be captured or killed ... or captured and killed. The day that John André again crosses my threshold will be the day when I know this war is lost."

Peggy is sobbing, but Edward Shippen does not skip a beat, saying, "Now, as for the main subject: Major Benedict Arnold. Two weeks from now, you will show him a good time, my dear. He is a hero among the colonies. He is a widower. He is eligible. You have my permission to flirt with him, Peggy. No, you have my insistence upon flirting him. Do you understand?"

Peggy, disturbed by her father's making short shrift of her "Johnny" and with tears still in her eyes, does not reply.

9

Edward Shippen, now in a louder voice, says, "You are my only daughter yet unwed. I want you out of my house. Don't you know that?"

Peggy looks at her father through moist eyes, but does not answer him.

Judge Shippen does not lessen the volume of his rant, saying, "You, Peggy Shippen, are not even engaged. In fact, you have had no men callers at all. I will not have you single any longer. Do you understand me? Do you understand about the flirting with Benedict Arnold? Answer me!"

"Yes, Father," she whimpers. "I shall do as you ask."

Edward Shippen pats his daughter's shoulder and says, "That's my girl. It will all be for the best."

Mr. Shippen leaves his daughter's side and moves toward the doorway. He calls over his shoulder, "But you dare not address Major Benedict Arnold as *Benny.*"

CHAPTER 3

Spies, Spies, and More Spies

The Colonial Army might not have a spymaster like Colonel John André, but they do have the Culper Ring. And it is growing. The earliest members of the ring, of course, have been Benjamin Tallmadge (a.k.a. John Bolton), Abraham Woodhull (a.k.a. Samuel Culper), and Robert Townsend (a.k.a. Samuel Culper Jr.).

Recently added to the list have been some new names, and of course, some new aliases. Austin Roe, a Long Island land courier, has become Agent 724, and Caleb Brewster, a Long Island Sound sea courier, has been given the code number 725.

There are other minor players, but these five—Tallmadge, Woodhull, Townsend, Roe, and Brewster—form the hub of the ring. Of these, Benjamin Tallmadge, at age twenty-three, is the youngest. For security reasons, the identities of most of the members of the ring are unknown to the other members. Typically, one of the spies knows the name of one—but no more than two—of the other spies.

In July 1778, the Culper Ring's first mission begins. The relay of that particular secret message transpires in New Jersey, New York City, Long Island, Long Island Sound, and its neighboring Connecticut shore. The networking proves to take several days.

Austin Roe, later to acquire the nickname "The Paul Revere of Long Island," is a Long Island tavern owner who often takes his wagon into New

11

York City on the pretense of buying goods for his tavern. On this particular day, a Tuesday, Roe and his wagon enter the city. He seeks out Robert Townsend, at Townsend's coffeehouse at the end of Wall Street. There, he stops his wagon and posts his horse. He enters the shop.

"Good day, sir," Austin Roe greets Townsend, behind his bar.

"Good day to you," the storeowner replies. "Can I be of help?"

"A black coffee would suit me well." Roe scans the premises. "Am I your only customer?"

"Aye, and my last. I am about to close." Robert Townsend walks from behind the bar to the wall that fronts the street and lowers the window shade. He does likewise at the front door, which he then locks and pockets the key. He points to the store's rear wall doorway, and both men exit to climb the stairs to Townsend's private loft. There is no time for the coffee transaction. They sit at the kitchen table.

Roe retrieves a large quill pen from his coat pocket and hands it to Townsend.

"What's this?" asks Robert.

"Inside the pen is the message. You may extract it from the hollow end at the point."

Townsend examines the feather quill, turning it over and over in his hands. He tries but cannot get the concealed paper to budge. "My nails are bitten off. Yours are longer—you do it."

With the nails of his forefinger and thumb Austin Roe pulls on the quill's contents, and the skinny, rolled, paper cylinder slides into his grasp. He hands it to Robert Townsend.

As Townsend unwinds the rolled paper, he asks, "I've not seen this done before. Who did it?"

"Number 725 handed it to me, straight from his boat, he didn't say—"

"And don't dare tell me either. I don't know this 725, don't want to, and don't want to know how or from whom he got it. I shouldn't have asked."

"It looks blank," observes Roe. "Has 725 sent us a dummy?"

"We'll soon see." Townsend stands, opens a cupboard door, and retrieves a vial.

"Is that the reagent?"

Robert nods. "Let's see if it works." Using a gob of cotton to soak up a quantity of the liquid from the glass vial, Robert smears the fluid up and down the narrow white paper. Both men look at it.

"There it is, the white ink," announces Austin Roe.

They silently read the exposed message.

Roe says, "So, the old man wants to know what General Clinton's up to. Why's the commander so interested in Saratoga, anyway, Robert?"

"Not for us to know, not for us to care. But this one's easy, you see. Over coffee, I recently hear the redcoats are bored in this berg, bored of staying put, that is. My answer will use up very little of the invisible stain. I'm in short supply as it is.

Robert Townsend lifts one of his own quill pens from the table, immerses its tip into a bottle of "medicine" (General Washington's code name for the disappearing ink), and inscribes on George Washington's skinny message sheet: "No movement north, Humble Servant, 723." He hands the paper to Austin Roe and says, "Let it dry a minute, and you can probably reroll and fit this better than I can into your small quill point."

After a moment, Austin rerolls and reinserts the tiny paper into the pen and pockets it. "I must leave, Robert. I've got fifty-five miles to cover back to the sound."

After the two exchange a handshake, Roe descends the stairs and crosses the floor to open the door to the street. "It's locked," he calls back to Townsend.

"Here it is." Townsend, right behind Roe, waves the key, catches up to Austin, and unlocks the door. "Be safe, my friend, and by all means avoid the docks—too many officers there."

Austin Roe exits, enters the street, unties his horse from the hitch, boards his wagon, and is off.

Roe's exodus from the city is uneventful, as is his subsequent fifty-five-mile trek back to his Long Island town, Setauket. Upon arrival there—it is now Wednesday—he is disappointed to discover that his next contact, Number 724, Caleb Brewster, is unavailable.

Because of a prearranged signal that Roe and Agent 722 (Abraham Woodhull) have devised, Roe knows that Brewster is nowhere near. If Abraham Woodhull's wife were have to have hung on her clothesline a black petticoat, then that would indicate to Roe that Caleb Brewster and his boat were in town.

13

Austin Roe sees no petticoats at all on Mrs. Woodhull's line, so he steers his steed toward his tavern. He parks, enters, and puts himself to bed, awaiting tomorrow's sunrise.

On Thursday morning, Austin Roe rises, breakfasts, and saddles a different horse of his. He goes without a wagon, which would have slowed him down, and heads toward the Woodhull cottage.

When within sight of the Woodhull's backyard, he spies on the clothesline a black petticoat, flanked by four white handkerchiefs. Roe laughs aloud; he is pleased to know that Caleb Brewster has sailed his boat across Long Island Sound from Connecticut to Setauket.

Setauket has six separate inlets on the northern shore of Long Island. So, the spies have devised a numbering system for those coves: #1 to #6. Roe heads from town to the cove #4 as heralded by the number of white handkerchiefs on Mrs. Woodhull's clothesline.

Caleb Brewster's moored boat should be waiting for Austin Roe at inlet #4. Although Brewster's skiff has always allowed him to outrun any and all attempts by the British ship captains to intercept him, he nonetheless always seeks to conceal the location of his vessel when it is anchored.

Roe arrives at the cove and advances up to the sleek, single-masted, lightweight sloop anchored in shallow water.

Caleb Brewster spots the horseman and waves from the craft's stern. "Ahoy," he hollers.

"Ahoy, yourself." Austin Roe dismounts, removes his boots, and begins to wade toward the sloop.

Caleb Brewster lowers himself into the water and wades toward Roe.

"Here's the quill," Roe says as he hands over the pen.

"Is this the same one?"

"Same pen, same paper."

"Pinching his pences, is he, that number 723 friend of yours?"

"There were no instructions to do otherwise," explains Roe. "Besides, he's running low on the *medicine*, so he might be low on other materials as well."

"Then I'll post him some old goose feathers by courier."

"No, Caleb. You do the sailing—I'll do the mailing. You have serious business to conduct."

"Serious, indeed, but I'm bored. Those British Goliaths with sails can't get within two furlongs of this little sloop. They can't even make a chase of it. I'm so bored that I'd pluck the feathers from that goose myself—while the bird's still alive even."

"Caleb, set sail. We need you to get this to number 721, whoever the hell he is."

"Never you mind who 721 is. Maybe after this war I'll tell you about him ... and you can tell me how you knew which cove to find me in."

"Caleb, set sail, damn it!"

The seaman turns and strides through the shallow area of the sound to his craft as the horseman returns to his animal on land.

At their destinations, the two agents give each other a wave as Roe's horse begins to trot toward home and Caleb Brewster's sloop starts to cut into the Long Island Sound toward the Connecticut shore to the north.

The sailing distance for Brewster from Long Island to the town of Fairfield on the sound's northern shore is about twenty miles. After more than two hours, Caleb Brewster reaches that Connecticut town, where he anchors and wades ashore.

At Fairfield, Brewster makes a dead drop. The dead drop target is on the highest ground within sight of Brewster's landing spot on the sound, which Caleb now ascends on foot. There, he finds the target tree, the only hawthorn tree on the knoll.

At the tree, he reaches up to a hollowed-out broken branch that angles from the trunk up and off to Caleb's right. Caleb, on tiptoe, can just barely reach up to the top of the drilled-out, two-foot-long branch stub.

He removes the cork-like hardwood stopper at the upper tip of the branch, slides his plume pen down into the hollow of the branch, and re-caps the opening.

Caleb avoids the tree's thorn-induced cuts that he has experienced on several other dead-drop deliveries or pickups. The hawthorn's possession of thorny stems is one reason that Agent 722, Major Benjamin Tallmadge, has chosen that species for his dead drops at Fairfield—nosy children and others are more than likely to stay clear of the prickly, little thorns.

Caleb Brewster descends the hill, wades to his awaiting sloop, brings the anchor, and sets sail.

Major Benjamin Tallmadge, who is stationed in Fairfield at Black Rock

Fort on Grover's Hill, only has but a quarter-mile walk that he makes each morning and evening to the hawthorn tree's knoll to check for dead drops.

The next morning, Friday, Major Tallmadge does his daily walk to the rise to inspect the mount's only Crataegus tree. The major avoids the hawthorn's prickly branches, retrieves the quill from its hiding place, and extracts Brewster's message. Tallmadge replaces the hardwood stopper, reads the note, returns it into the plume, which he pockets, and returns to Black Rock Fort. There, the major dispatches the message by rider, a member of his dragoon unit.

After two nights of sleeping and three days on horseback, the dragoon messenger has by now forded the Hudson River and crossed from Connecticut westward into New Jersey. On Monday, the horseman arrives at General George Washington's headquarters at Morristown, New Jersey.

The dispatcher is escorted to General Washington's headquarters, which is a commandeered private citizen's house, and turns over the message-containing quill to the commander in chief.

It has taken six days for Washington's question to make it to its Culper Ring destination and another seven days for the network to have gotten the answer back to the general. Upon receipt of this quill message from Tallmadge's dragoon, the commander in chief is anything but pleased by the slowness of his spies.

Washington's reaction can be heard throughout most of the camp. "I need news in one night—not in a fortnight!"

CHAPTER 4
Fatherly Advice

Thirteen days ago, Judge Edward Shippen issued his insistence that his daughter engage in a flirtatious evening with Major Benedict Arnold at the dinner/ball scheduled for the Shippen mansion.

Today, Shippen says, "What are your plans for tomorrow evening's event, Peggy?"

"Do you wish me to be the kind of flirt that you demanded my sister to be?"

"Ah, but that demand met with much success, did it not? She married into wealth, as shall you soon—to the famous Major Arnold."

"What makes you so certain of my marriage to him?"

"Our family is influential, Peggy, more influential than you realize. A Shippen lass would be a feather in the cap of any gentleman of position. And a lass of your beauty would appeal to any man of his age, particularly to a widower such as Arnold who has been without conjugal intimacy for a time now."

"Father, your language startles me so."

"Become accustomed to it, my dear. We are about to do ... that is, you are about to do whatever it takes to seize this prize."

"But, Father, how is that you are aware of the gentleman's intimacies?"

"Lack of intimacies, my love, the lack of them."

"Well, lack of intimacies, then. How can you be so certain?"

"Peggy, I am no pauper. This is my city. Let us just say that I have my spies."

17

"I am not as certain as are you about all of this, Father. And though my heart is not in it, you know that I shall do your bidding. By the by, have you any boundaries set for my honeying up to Mr. Arnold?"

"You honey up all you want, love, but remember, you want the major just to taste your sweetness—not to satiate his appetite."

"Is contact ... I mean, is touching permitted?"

"Of course, and this might take days, Peggy, but for now, you may arouse him however you might, promise him however much you wish, but his promise to you in return must be a proposal, with whatever time it takes for him to do that."

"May I wear my *cutaway* blouse?"

"Your what?"

"It's the one I scissored from the neck down to here." Her index finger presses against the bottom of her sternum. I shaped it for my love, Colonel André."

"Peggy, Peggy, I have cautioned you more than once to forget all about this André—and with a name like that, he must be French or Flemish anyway. Forget him—just remember that your new love is a true American."

"And what do I gain from my transacting with this true American?"

"You get to obey your father is what you get."

"What if I were to ask you, Father, if my transaction with Mr. Arnold might not lead to my getting a lovely honeymoon and my getting a lovely palace to return to from the honeymoon?"

Edward Shippen laughs, thinks on it a moment, and says, "I'll say this much, Peggy, I can arrange a postwedding trip for you and Major Arnold to one of our several moneyed relatives. And, by the way, you do like the manor house at Mount Pleasant, do you not?"

"The one overlooking the river, up on the cliff that Captain ... Captain something-or-other is selling?"

"The very one, built by Captain John Macpherson. It's yours ... if you can rope Arnold."

Peggy smiles. "I do not love this Major Arnold, Father, but consider him roped, tied, and branded."

CHAPTER 5

The (Brief) Courtship of Peggy and Benedict

Later in July, the big day arrives, the day for the dinner dance at the Shippen mansion. As the guests arrive, the Shippens' servants direct them to their respective seats.

Peggy, near the entrance of the great room, says, "Find your name tag on your table. Remember, it's boy-girl, boy-girl, boy-girl, etcetera."

In actuality, a scorekeeper would easily have noted that the Shippens have invited several more males than females to the party. That contrivance is, of course, to lessen the potential demand upon Major Arnold—demand by females other than Peggy Shippen, that is. When the evening's dancing begins, the surplus of males will leave no female unattended. Peggy and her father have reduced the field of competitors—subtraction by addition.

At the dinner, of course, Benedict Arnold is assigned to be seated beside Peggy. His chair will be at the head end of a four-foot-by-six-foot table, which is dwarfed by the dimensions of the other tables in the grand room. The table is void of chairs, except for one seat for Arnold and one for Peggy—a table conducive to quiet conservation. So much for Edward Shippen's seating chart.

Peggy is seated before Arnold arrives at the table. Benedict, only partially recovered from battle wounds, is on crutches. He has been unable to find his name on any other table and observes that the seat beside Peggy is the only one in the great room remaining unoccupied. "I trust that this seat is mine?" he asks.

"It most certainly is." Peggy extends her hand toward the major. Arnold steadies himself with one crutch clenched under his right armpit, his left hand clasping the other crutch. With his free right hand, he lifts her outstretched fingers to gently press the upper surface of Peggy's hand to his lips.

"Good day to you, Miss … Miss Shippen?"

"Yes."

"I was unable to find my assigned place, and as I approached from the other end of the table. I could not make out a *Benedict* or an *Arnold* on this sheet." He points to the paper near his tableware. "So, I was still unsure, seeing as how the paper reads *Hero of Philadelphia*." He chuckles.

"But, sir, you are our hero, the only hero this town has left."

"But I have not fought here. My battles have been elsewhere. My wounds have not been inflicted anywhere near Pennsylvania." He slides his crutches onto the floor behind his chair, places one hand on the table and the other on the arm of his chair, and lowers himself into his seat.

"But your wounds and your gallantry at Ticonderoga and at Saratoga are legend, Major. You are our hero, sir … well, at least you indeed are mine."

"Indeed?" he asks.

"Why yes, indeed. I have felt thus about you even before meeting you. Now that I have met you, I am quite satisfied with myself that I have chosen so handsome and athletic a man as my hero."

"Miss Shippen, you flatter me."

"What would flatter me, would be for you to kindly reserve me as your partner in this evening's first dance."

"But as you see … my crutches … they, they will not permit me much freedom of movement. I fear that I will be unable to fulfill your wish."

By now, all guests have been seated and served and are beginning to partake.

Peggy says, "Well, you could brace yourself on your sticks, and I could dance around you … around you, perhaps somewhat … perhaps somewhat against you."

Arnold smiles and laughs. "And indeed I might have to brace myself, if I heard you correctly, my dear. Am I mistaken, did you or did you not say you could dance *against* me?"

"I might have said 'dance against you,' or I might have said 'dance again with you.' Which is it that you would prefer me to have said, sir?"

"A gentleman might choose not to be so forward as to answer so pleasing a question from so pleasing a young lady, Miss Peggy."

"Pleasing ... in this old thing?" She caresses her cutaway blouse where its fabric touches her bosom.

"My dear, I see no old thing. I see such a young and beautiful thing."

"Sir, your language within the minute has progressed from my being pleasing to my being beautiful. I can promise you, Major, that if I can take you at your word that I am beautiful, then you can take me at my word that I can also be pleasing. That is, if you could grant me the privilege of pleasing you, of course. Are you interested, Major, in progressing with me this evening in more than words, but also in deeds?"

Arnold, surprised by the young woman's forwardness and taken aback by her suggestive request, does not—or cannot—answer.

Peggy waits for a response. Hearing none, she continues, "Your silence only leaves me to guess just how our dancing might progress, sir, whether it shall be 'again with you' or 'against you.'" She smiles.

A rush of vascular red emanating from his face, the thunderstruck Benedict still is silent.

Peggy resumes her prodding, saying, "I want more than just your time, sir. I wish for our evening to become more intimate ... as intimate as you might desire it to become."

Peggy's provocative insinuating has fallen upon the ears of a mature gentleman—twice the age of the questioning lass—but the man cannot manage an answer any more than he can manage to contain his involuntary, fevered blush.

Peggy is relentless, saying, "Not only do you govern this city, Major Arnold, but you could also govern me. I will do your bidding."

Arnold finally brings himself to answer the enchantress, "I must say, Miss Peggy, that I do not quite understand, but I also must say that I am quite interested. Exactly what is it that you are proposing?"

"Not in this hall, sir, but upstairs, I will—"

"But I have been invited here to enjoy the luxury and comfort of this hall, downstairs. It would be a display of rudeness for me to leave—"

"The rudeness, Mr. Benedict Arnold, would lie in your refusal to accommodate me, your hostess, for the evening."

"I could not bring myself to be rude toward you, Miss Peggy. What words might I offer to convince you of that?"

"Actions speak louder, they say," Peggy says. "It is the bringing of yourself to the second floor that is the action I am asking."

"My best excuse for not doing so, Miss Peggy is my crutches. You see, on the stairs, it would be difficult for me to—"

"If that is your best excuse, sir, then rest assured, we can get you upstairs."

"We?"

"I am quite friends with my maid, Laura, actually. She and I have an arrangement. I have overlooked her liaisons on second floor with her gentleman friend, and she is eager to assist me with my planned naughtiness with you. I scratch her back, as they say ... she will do what is necessary for you to help me with my itch, Benedict."

Arnold partly swallows and partly coughs at his last bite of his meal. "Naughtiness? Your itch? But in your parents' house, surely you cannot mean—"

"I mean to welcome you to our house ... a special welcome. My parents shall be preoccupied with their many guests and for many hours. My upstairs room is secure and comfortable. Laura and I can get you there. I will supply you with a more comfortable wardrobe, and I promise to run from you so slowly that—with or without your crutches—you may take me prisoner."

Major Benedict Arnold had expected to attend this South Fourth Street party to enjoy a meal with the Shippens and hear some fine music. He had not expected the sort of welcome that Peggy is promising. But the hearing of the seductive overtures from the tantalizing Miss Shippen and mulling them over in his mind render Arnold as defenseless as a love-stricken male mantis in the clutches of his female mate.

Benedict says, "Miss Shippen, I must ask, when you suggest that I may help you with your itch and take you prisoner, are your words the mere rhetorical hospitality of a hostess or are they the words of a willing partner in intimacy? If I might be so bold as to ask."

"My dear Major, my suggestion to you is not rhetorical, and be assured that it is more than a suggestion. Please be aware that I promise to you unconditional surrender, sir. I invite you, nay I implore you, to be as bold with me as you please. And be assured that the pleasure, Benedict Arnold, will be mine."

The evening's dining has been fine for Arnold, but he sees that Peggy is offering something much finer. "Well, how can we depart from your other guests without being impolite?"

"The guests will be being entertained by my parents. There shall be no notice. Laura and a trusted manservant shall escort you upstairs."

"And you shall follow?"

"I shall run."

"You are able to run in those long skirts?"

"I can lift my skirts to my knee to hurry up the stairs. And be assured, I can lift my skirts higher, that is, if you command it."

Command it? What am I doing still seated at this table? He grabs his crutches from behind him and rises. Peggy has already beckoned the maid and servant to Arnold's chair. The major, unnoticed by any other eyes, makes his way to the nearby stairs and—with Laura and the servant's aid—climbs them.

Laura leads Arnold into Peggy's bedroom and retrieves one of Judge Shippen's dressing gowns from a closet. She hands it to the major and smiles. "Miss Peggy said that you would know what to do with this."

Arnold nods and takes the article of clothing from the maid, whose smile is broadening.

Laura, now giggling, leaves, shutting the door behind her. Benedict disrobes down to his underwear, lays his outer garments on a chair, and dons the robe.

Benedict sits on the bed, resting his crutches against the bedstead. *What shall I command this prisoner of mine to do first?*

Soon he hears a knock at the door. He rises, picks up his crutches, and walks to the door. When he opens it, and sees there a Shippen—but not Peggy Shippen. Instead, it is Judge Edward Shippen.

Whether or not Peggy's father has a shotgun in hand is unclear, but what is clear is that Edward Shippen immediately extracts from Benedict Arnold: a confession, a marriage proposal, and a wedding date.

CHAPTER 6

The (Brief) Honeymoon of Peggy and Benedict

The gentleman's contract made in July between Judge Shippen and Major Arnold for Benedict's betrothal to Peggy Shippen is about to be honored. The two men have set the wedding date for April 8 of the upcoming year.

That day arrives, and the thirty-eight-year-old Arnold is wed to eighteen-year-old Peggy Shippen. April proves to be a rain-filled month, and the newlyweds spend an inordinate quantity of time indoors—even for a honeymoon.

After a brief, wet sojourn at Shippen family homes in Pennsylvania and New Jersey, the couple returns to the Philadelphia area to the equally wet Mount Pleasant manor house. After the one o'clock meal, Mrs. Peggy Arnold says, "I'm tired of so much rain and so much inactivity."

"Can you not find another book to read? The library has its fill," the major says.

"And I too have had a fill of books these past five days. Can we not invite some guests?"

"You are well aware, are you not, Peggy, of my resumption of duties here in your fair city. And are you not also well aware of the pile of correspondence to which I must now respond? For instance, Peggy, there are the vendors, other purveyors, inferior officers, superior officers ... spies ... all of whom demand my reply."

"Spies?"

"Aye, for a while now, I've been wanting to tell someone. The commander in chief has entrusted me to set up a small group of spies. General Washington needs some Pennsylvania eyes and ears to augment those that he has already stationed in New York.

"Washington has insisted that I recruit my snoopers exclusively from among Philadelphia's citizenry, but only those who have all appearances of being Loyalists. In fact, your father has joined me and has brought a few of his fellows along."

"Spies? My father? How intriguing. Show me."

"Show you what?"

"Why, the spy correspondence, of course."

"You don't understand, my sweet. The Philadelphia spy correspondence is secret and must remain secret. You cannot ask me to divulge—"

"Should a newly married husband and wife have secrets from one another? Is that a way to start a marriage, Ben?"

Arnold rises from his chair, walks toward the door, and enters the adjoining room.

"Where are you going?"

"I'll be back. I just might have something for you." After a moment, Ben returns with an envelope. "I suppose that it's safe to let you see a message that should make no sense at all to you. It's encrypted."

"Encrypted?"

"Our spies' secret ciphering, and I shall need the note back again this evening after my napping." He hands the envelope to her. "See if this can relieve your boredom, Peggy. See if you can makes heads or tails of it."

Peggy accepts the envelope, opens it, removes the letter, and glances at the message. "But there are no words here—just numbers. Can I not have one with real words?"

"They are real enough, my dear. After I have relayed this very message to the commander in chief—and after we have acted upon it—I shall perhaps then feel free to tell you a word or two from the whole of it."

"Never you bother. I'm convinced that you shall tell me little if anything about your precious little secrets. Go. Take your nap."

Peggy lays the letter and its envelope on the table as Benedict yawns, stretches both arms skyward, and says, "I'll see you after my sleep."

Peggy spreads the letter flat on the table top, eyes it for a second time, and thinks, *He believes that I cannot decipher. I'll figure this out and show him when he awakes.*

She immediately notices a vague similarity between this message before her and messages like it that she and her beloved Colonel John Andre had exchanged in the past.

She also realizes that what she fails to possess is a key word to permit decoding. Her key word with Colonel André has always been *Philadelphia*, from which just the first three letters—the P, the H, and the I—were useful in the deciphering.

She decides to try to discover her husband's key word that he uses with his spies. *But where to look?* Peggy's first thought is the epaulets on her husband's dress uniform, Benedict always having been so particular about their cleaning and combing.

Peggy walks past their bedroom and hears Benedict's snoring. A few feet beyond that, she reaches his suit, which is hanging in the hallway.

Ruffling through his uniform's epaulets and feeling their attachment points to the coat's shoulders, she finds nothing. As an afterthought, she reaches her hands into both coat pockets and withdraws a small sheet of paper in each hand.

On one sheet is written: "ODD—GEORGE WASHINGTON." On the other is written: "EVEN—JOHN ADAMS." Peggy repeats the words to herself a few times, committing them to memory, and returns the papers to their respective pockets of Benedict's uniform. She retraces her steps back past Ben—still asleep—to the dining table.

At the table, Peggy reexamines Ben's encrypted spy letter. Because she and John André have never used "odd" or "even" in their coded messages, she is stumped. *Could the code words mean the odd or even day, week, or month of the year that the note is dated? On the odd day, week, or month, the spies could have used George Washington as the key, but on even days, weeks, or months, the spies could have used the John Adams key.*

From her experience with encrypted messages, Peggy is able to mentally try those alternatives in attempting to decipher just the first word of Benedict's spy message, but to no avail. The calendar date seems not to be the key.

Peggy's next idea is to assume that the *odd* and *even* would mean the odd or even number of words in the paragraph. She counts ten words in the message and begins a mental deciphering based upon that even number. Ten could signify the possible use by the spies of the first letters of John Adams's name—accompanied by the word "even"—as the possible key.

Her visual conception of the first word's several letters proves to be a failure. *Well, if* odd *and* even *don't mean the number of words, perhaps they mean the number of lines in the paragraph. This message has three lines. Let's try* odd.

It takes a while and a little ink sketching of a chart on a scrap piece of paper, but to her delight, Peggy sees that by noting the odd number of lines in the spy message and by using the beginning of George Washington's name (GEO) as the key, that the first seven letters in her husband's spy letter probably form a real, intelligible word: W-A-R-N-I-N-G.

So she begins to work on the message's second word and discovers that those five letters also make sense: I-R-I-S-H. Then she proceeds to attack the remaining eight words.

Continuing to use her chart, Peggy solves all ten words. On a separate paper, Peggy writes out the entire message:

WARNING—IRISH DESERTER
IN HIS EXCELLENCY'S GUARD
IS THE KIDNAPPER.

Peggy pockets her copy of the note along with her sketched chart.

When her husband rises from his afternoon nap, he asks, "Did you make anything of the numbers?"

"Indeed. I did so."

"So, what does it tell you?"

"It tells me that His Excellency, King George, shall be kidnapped and shipped to Ireland."

"Congratulations, my dear. How were you able to do that?"

"My secret, Ben. You have your secrets—I have mine."

A chuckling Arnold says, "So be it, so be it, my darling." As his chuckle turns to laughter, he pauses, leans toward Peggy, and gently presses his lips upon her brow.

"Why do you laugh at me?" she asks.

Withdrawing a few inches from his kiss, Benedict says, "Sweet Peggy, you are only correct insofar that there is a George to be kidnapped, all right, but the Excellency in the message is His Excellency, General George Washington."

"Your commander-in-chief?"

"The very one."

"And your spy is informing you?"

"Nay, it is I who is informing Washington's staff."

"So, the writing in the note is yours."

"Aye, and fess up, just how were you able to decipher it?"

"I could only guess, I mean only guess that the *GEO* in *George Washington* might be the key."

"And how is it that you come to know so much about cryptography and about such a thing as a key?"

"We ... I mean I and a former acquaintance of mine once undertook such sport just for amusement."

"Well, be that as it may, I should put you to use then. I mean, you might spare me quite some time in the ciphering and deciphering of incoming and outgoing dispatches—if you're up to it, that is."

"You do know that I truly have been bored of late. I would be so pleased to be of assistance to you, Ben."

"I hesitate to impose upon you, Peggy, but your help with the cryptography should permit me to see to the other assorted tasks and duties with which this Philadelphia governance burdens me."

"Dear Ben, you must realize that a husband's burden is a wife's burden too. We shall share."

Benedict again softly lays a kiss upon her forehead and says, "Then it is settled."

As she hands Benedict the envelope and note, Peggy asks, "Shall I do anything more with this letter?"

"Nothing at all. I'm to send it by morning courier off to Morristown."

"Morristown?"

"Aye, General Washington's headquarters at the Ford Mansion there. I should seal this envelope and package it for the courier."

"Dear, I might stroll the garden whilst you do your readying for delivery."

He nods.

Peggy walks to the front door and exits the mansion.

Ben takes the envelope and its contents toward the library.

Outdoors, Peggy lifts from her pocket her copy of the spy note and her sketched chart. Reading and rereading the two sheets, Peggy smiles. *My boredom is vanishing. I am becoming a cryptographer. Perhaps the commander in chief just might want to be my pen friend.*

CHAPTER 7
Morristown's Ford Mansion

It is two days later, and the scene is Morristown, New Jersey. The Continental Army encampment occupies hundreds of acres, elevated on defensible terrain, and on a crossroads of critical communication routes. Commander-in-Chief Washington's headquarters is the almost brand-new Ford Mansion, built by Jacob and Theodosia Ford between 1772 and 1774.

General Washington is in the field with several of his lieutenants when a pair of horseback riders arrives at the mansion. The riders dismount and are escorted to Captain Alexander Hamilton, commander pro tem of the mansion in General Washington's absence.

Each rider hands Captain Hamilton an envelope and leave the mansion.

Hamilton immediately takes the envelopes to his office, opens them, removes the long, folded paper sheet from each, and unfolds and flattens them on his desk-top. In minutes, Hamilton has deciphered both messages, transcribing them onto two smaller paper sheets of his own.

When General Washington returns from the field, Alexander Hamilton is waiting on the front porch. He hands both of his small sheets to Washington and says, "What do you make of these?"

Perusing the three lines on each sheet, George Washington says, "Obviously, they confirm each other. We must take this warning seriously. Do we have an Irishman among us?"

"Aye, sir, a Sergeant Thomas Hickey—one of your lifeguards—deserted the Irish to join us."

"Captain, round up the Irishman."

"I already have taken the liberty to do so. I sent two infantrymen to bring Hickey here. Did I not do the right thing?"

"Perfectly the right thing. We shall hang this Thomas Hickey. Here, file these." George hands the two letters to Alexander Hamilton. "Why is it that we have two copies of the message? Did Arnold send duplicates?"

"I'm not certain, sir, I recognized Arnold's courier from Philadelphia, but I did not recognize the other rider."

"Two riders?"

"Aye, and two different signatures, did you notice?"

Washington takes back the two papers from Hamilton and eyes them. "I expect this from Arnold—too proud to use a pen name—but this other one, this number 711, it looks somewhat familiar. Is 711 one of our New York ring?"

"Not that I'm aware of. As far as I know, our Culpers thus far have only used the numbers 721 through 725 as their calling cards. Perhaps 711 is a new recruit of theirs."

"Nonetheless, we have Arnold's and this other sympathizer's word—whoever he is. We can douse this kidnapping conspiracy before it is lit."

"Conspiracy? Do you suspect others among us?"

"Aye, Alexander. Conspiracy loves company, as they say."

Hamilton frowns.

Washington adds, "Well, conspiracy loves company is what they should say, Alexander."

Captain Hamilton offers a belated chuckle and asks, "How shall we find out?"

"We need to question Hickey—and see if he will lead us to the others."

Within the hour, two soldiers from Washington's infantry bring Thomas Hickey, in chains, to General Washington at the commander's mansion office. Alexander Hamilton accompanies them.

General Washington says, "Are these the shackles which bound him at the jail?"

"Yes, sir," answers one of the soldiers.

"Will you unbind him please?"

The other infantryman removes a key from his pocket and unlocks the prisoner's leg cuffs. "The handcuffs as well?"

Washington nods, and the soldier frees Thomas Hickey's hands.

"Please be seated, Mr. Hickey."

Thomas sits.

The general continues, "I wish you to be comfortable, Thomas, so that we might talk."

Hickey is silent, but his eyes remain riveted on his inquisitor.

Washington, showing Hickey one of the messages deciphered by Alexander Hamilton, asks, "Do you see these lines? Are you able to read them?"

"Yes, sir."

"What does 'The Irish deserter in His Excellency's guard is the kidnapper' mean?

"I don't know, sir."

"Well, is it true that you, Thomas Hickey, are Irish?"

"Yes, sir."

Is it true that you are a deserter?"

"No, sir. I am not."

"I shall rephrase. Have you ever in your life been a deserter?"

"Well ... uh ... well, yes, sir, from His Majesty's Royal Army."

"And have you served in my bodyguard."

"I am in it at this very moment, sir."

"So, you are a kidnapper?"

"No, sir. I am not."

"Again, I shall rephrase. Have you ever been a kidnapper?"

"No, sir. I have not."

"Well, do you ever plan to be a kidnapper?"

Hickey does not answer.

"I repeat, are you to be a kidnapper in the future?"

No response.

The general proceeds, "We know that there is a kidnapping conspiracy. Are you part of it?"

Hickey remains silent.

"Thomas, if you give us some names, I shall do what I can to lessen the severity of your punishment."

The prisoner begins to part his lips as if to speak, but then closes them.

Washington says, "Thomas, you name some names, and your lockup shall be no longer than a few months. How say you?"

Hickey finally says, "They will kill me, sir."

"Who will kill you, Thomas?"

"The other guardsmen when I am released or the other conspirators if I tell on them, that's who."

"So, you admit that there are other conspirators then?"

Hickey lowers his head, eyes to the ground, and returns to silence.

Washington says, "Let me ask you, Thomas, will you tell me who the conspiracy leaders are if I tell you that, in return, I shall set you free?"

Hickey looks up. "Free to do what? Free to go where, sir? I fear that if I tell what you wish to hear, I shall become an outcast to both sides in this conflict."

"Would your freedom and a guaranteed safe passage to your homeland suffice?"

Thomas smiles for the first time. "You will ship me to Ireland, sir?"

"You have my word." George reaches his hand to Thomas, who studies the general's hand for a second or two and then grasps it in a handshake. Washington resumes the interrogation, saying, "Who has organized this kidnap plot?"

"I know only of two, and I have heard only their last names, sir."

"Come forth, come forth. Last names will do."

"I am certain only of a Mr. Tryon and a Mr. Matthews. I—"

Captain Alexander Hamilton says, "Might those gentlemen be Governor William Tryon and Mayor David Matthews?"

"Seems as be that I recollect the one bein' sometimes called *Gov*, but I never heard the other one bein' called anything save Matthews."

Hamilton looks at Washington, and Washington nods.

As the captain turns and heads toward the doorway, the general says, "Round them up!"

Washington turns to the two infantrymen. "Lock Hickey back up and to the cellar with him."

Hickey says, "But, General, you gave your word. You promised I was to be free."

"Indeed I have. And indeed you shall be free, Thomas. This lockup is but temporary. It is for your own protection until I can arrange for your safe passage home."

Hickey nods as the soldiers chain him and escort him away.

When the room is empty, General Washington shrugs and says, "One of my own bodyguards has betrayed me. Whom can I trust?"

CHAPTER 8

The Brief Stay of Peggy and Benedict at Mount Pleasant

At Philadelphia's Mount Pleasant, Benedict receives a return message from General Washington's headquarters. He reads it and calls out, "Peggy, can you come here?

Peggy calls back from the hallway, "I'm coming." She joins Benedict in their library, walks to his chair, and asks, "What is it?"

"Look at this." He hands her the letter. It is not encrypted.

She reads it aloud.

My dear Major Arnold,

Your earlier notice to me regarding the Irishman's kidnapping plot has been most instrumental in foiling the enemy's plan. The confession of the conspirator, one Thomas Hickey, has led to the arrest of the chief villains in the plot. The episode too has alerted me to the necessity for a tighter security among my bodyguards. To that end, I have reassigned you to the newly established position of commander of the lifeguards.

Your new duties will require the exodus of you and yours from Philadelphia to Morristown, posthaste. Your

37

replacement as military governor shall soon be named. Needless to say, your new assignment will be accompanied by an increase in compensation.

The partitioning of a substantial section of Ford Mansion for the living quarters for you and Mrs. Arnold have already begun.

Awaiting your swift arrival,
General George Washington, commander in chief, Continental Army

Benedict exclaims, "More prestige, my darling, more money, and having the privilege of residing in the same building with His Excellency. Now this war is finally getting somewhere."

"I am so happy for you, Ben. I'm so happy for us. What shall I pack?"

"One of everything that we have—but only our finest, Peggy. Morristown is more than a hub of transportation. It is a hub of wealth and elegance. We shall turn that mansion into a party hall, a ballroom."

CHAPTER 9
General Clinton's Currency Scheme

Benedict and Peggy Arnold have had more than a month to settle comfortably into the Ford Mansion. Their living quarters have proven to be of sufficient space and have afforded sufficient privacy.

Benedict Arnold is proving to rule Washington's lifeguards with a stern discipline that had been lacking heretofore, but there exists no sign of even a possibility for a breach in security within that guard.

Peggy has continued to relieve Benedict of some of his responsibilities by continuing her pen and paper practice from their Philadelphia days.

On this day in early June 1779, after an early lunch, Peggy is deciphering the latest letter, which will soon be relayed to General Washington.

> General Clinton plans to steal in Philadelphia the paper from which Colonial currency is printed in order to flood colonies with worthless paper money, devalue currency, and degrade colonists' morale.
>
> Your faithful servant,
> 711

Peggy had sent a servant to request the presence of Captain Alexander Hamilton, the acting commander of the headquarters, while Benedict Arnold assists General Washington with reviewing troops in the field.

Captain Hamilton arrives at the Arnold's living quarters and says, "Good day, Madame Arnold. May I be of service?"

"Good day, Captain Hamilton. Perhaps you can. I am uncertain as to whether this recently received cipher from Philadelphia is worthy of General Washington's immediate attention or not. My husband is absent from the mansion, and I wondered if you might not wish to see it." She hands Hamilton both the original message and her plain English version.

Hamilton glances at the cipher and carefully reads its translation. "You certainly were right to call for me, Mrs. Arnold. We mustn't allow General Clinton to get his hands on our currency paper. I'm riding immediately to inform His Excellency. Let us hope that this message has arrived in time for us to act."

Hamilton bids Peggy goodbye, strides toward the exit door, and calls back to her, "Thank you, Madame. And thank your husband for having you do this deciphering for us."

Captain Hamilton locates General Washington and Major Arnold on their way back to the mansion headquarters for the noon meal. The two horsemen stop and greet the captain, and he turns over the two sheets from Peggy Arnold.

George Washington needs hardly any time to read the message. "Benedict, as quickly as possible, take as many of my bodyguards as you need. Fly to Philadelphia. Secure our warehouse's supply of currency print at all costs and send me immediate word of your success."

Major Arnold salutes his commander, turns his horse, and spurs him toward the barracks of the commander in chief's guard. He orders his lieutenant, Scott Anderson, to gather fifteen of his guardsmen and begin to execute the preparations for the mission.

Arnold turns his horse toward the mansion. At the mansion, Benedict dismounts, enters the building, and makes his way to his living quarters.

Arnold greets Peggy and briefly describes his orders from General Washington. The two pack up some of Benedict's personals.

Peggy says, "Ben, I'll join you in a moment. There are some goodies I wish to add to your pack."

Benedict, pack in hand, waits for the guard lieutenant and the other soldiers on the front porch.

Minutes later, Peggy joins him and adds two small containers to his pack. "I thought you might have use for a little jerky and some cookies."

"I'll put both to use, my dear, and happily."

With the guard squad not yet in sight, Benjamin takes the opportunity to congratulate Peggy. "Fortunate it has been for me and for His Excellency that you have become our best cryptographer."

Peggy offers a blushing smile and says, "And fortunate also that this new Agent 711—whoever he may be—is on our side. And by the way, 711's messages thus far have been relatively easy. I mean, he always uses the GEO or the JOH key. If he ever sends anything more sinuous, Ben, I just might need your assistance."

When Lieutenant Anderson and the other guard squad arrive, Ben kisses Peggy's cheek, mounts his horse, and joins the lieutenant at the head of the parade. He calls back to Peggy, "I'll write you when I write His Excellency."

The couple wave to one another, and the squad, descends the knoll.

Mrs. Arnold, still waving, calls out, "Be safe."

CHAPTER 10
The Philadelphia Warehouse

After a day's ride, Major Arnold, his lieutenant, and their squad of fifteen guards arrive at the Continental Army's Philadelphia storehouse, which is housing the prime-quality paper for printing Colonial currency.

As they near the warehouse, Lieutenant Anderson, at the point of the column of horsemen, calls out, "A guard, sir, I see a guard at the building."

Arnold spurs his horse to take the lead. Benedict arrives at the guard's position, dismounts, and asks, "Where are the others?"

"What others, sir?"

"The others guarding the building, of course."

"I am the only one, sir."

"The only one?" Benedict utters some mild oath under his breath just as the entire line of guardsmen arrives. Arnold says, "Fall in with the other fifteen here. You are now one of us."

Arnold and Lieutenant Anderson enter the ancient abandoned barn with various-sized wisps of hay strewn upon the dirt floor and the loft. Seeing that the reams of the precious paper appear to be in place and accounted for, both officers exit the building.

Outside, Arnold issues some orders. He and Lieutenant Anderson now have sixteen men in their charge. Daily, there is to be a pair of men stationed at each of the building's outside four walls, while the other eight guardsmen will be inside the warehouse. The indoor soldiers and the outdoor soldiers will trade places every eight hours.

Lieutenant Anderson is to patrol the building's entire exterior perimeter on horseback for eight hours, to be relieved by Arnold for four hours, followed by the lieutenant's next eight-hour turn, and so on.

Three days go by. Arnold, sitting inside, hears a gunshot from the building's exterior beyond its east wall. Benedict orders two soldiers, both privates, to open the doors at the east end and investigate the noise. Arnold instructs four of the other men to vacate the building via the west door: a pair to circle clockwise and a pair to circle counterclockwise to maneuver toward the direction of the firing.

The remaining two guardsmen are to stay near the stacked reams of paper.

The major joins the two privates at the east door and peers over the shoulder of one of the young men. The other private is pointing to a distant flash of red. "They're on foot, and they're running off," he calls out.

"Hold your fire," Benedict calls out to his lieutenant, who has brought his horse to the east end of the warehouse. "Take two men and follow them … as long as you must. Do not come back without worthwhile reconnaissance."

The lieutenant asks, "Should I not take more than two of us, sir?"

"No, this retreat of theirs could be just a ruse. We must guard against a second attack from a larger contingency."

"On foot or are we to take our horses?"

"On foot, but stay out of their view if possible—and, by all means, stay out of their range."

The three guardsmen follow the redcoats eastward.

Arnold redistributes his guard inside and outside the warehouse, leaving a somewhat stronger contingent at the exterior east wall. Benedict climbs the interior stairs to the loft, gaining a vantage point through its east-facing window.

About one hour later, Arnold sees his guard patrol returning. He descends to the first floor and exits the east door to meet his returning crew.

As the three soldiers near, Benedict calls out, "Report the enemy's status."

The lieutenant nears the major and says, "They're gone."

"Details, details," Arnold says.

Having arrived at his commanding officer's side, Anderson says, "There were only six of them, sir, only four armed, with the other two carrying large cloth baskets of a sort."

"Where are they now?"

"On the Delaware, Major, headed upstream in two canoes. Each canoe has two redcoats with paddles and one passenger holding a basket."

"No other army, no larger vessels?"

"None at least within leagues, as we could tell. My guess is that our presence surprised them. Judging from their hurried efforts against the Delaware's current, I believe that they shall not be returning."

The other two soldiers accompanying the lieutenant nod in agreement.

"Lieutenant, here is the letter I have just composed. It is to His Excellency, telling of our success. I shall burn the other contrary one. With all speed, get the letter to Morristown—by our same route here. Do you understand?"

"By all means, sir." Anderson mounts his horse and rides away.

To the guardsmen within earshot, Arnold says, "Get busy. Help the others pack up the currency paper. We're moving it to a safer place. I know just the spot."

CHAPTER 11

George Washington Shuffles the Deck

From Philadelphia, General Washington's guard lieutenant has ridden his horse—giving the animal short rest periods here and there—for about twelve hours and arrives at General Washington's Morristown encampment well past the general's bedtime. Because of the late hour, Lieutenant Anderson beds himself down for the night.

Upon rising, the lieutenant enters the mansion and is greeted by Captain Alexander Hamilton. Anderson turns over Benedict Arnold's letter from Philadelphia, and Hamilton maintains possession of the letter while waiting for General Washington to finish his morning meal. Then Hamilton approaches the still seated Commander.

Hamilton says, "This, sir, is from Major Arnold in Philadelphia." He hands the envelope to Washington.

The general opens it and reads the short note. "It appears that the currency paper is secure, for now. Thanks to our guard, Captain—and to our spies who uncovered the enemy's plot in the first place—I feel safe in saying that Clinton shall not be able to flood us with the worthless bills he had hoped to manufacture.

"Now put a message to Benedict into your own words, Captain. Summon him to return from Philadelphia immediately—but tell him to leave at least ten of my guards there to oversee the continued security of the paper. Come to think of it, send your note with Lieutenant Anderson. We'll leave him in charge of the Philadelphia men. They're his men anyway."

"Yes, sir." Captain Hamilton exits the general's dining area to compose the message for a courier.

It takes Anderson a day to get to Philadelphia and another day for Arnold to return to Morristown. Upon his return, Benedict immediately reports to General Washington.

Arnold approaches the general at his desk and notices that leaving Washington's desk is a soldier whom he recognizes by his uniform and face to be one of the dragoon dispatchers frequently a visitor to Washington at the Ford Mansion.

The dragoon and Benedict pass each other, and as Benedict reaches the General's desk, Washington is opening an envelope and starting to read its contents.

With his left hand raised and its palm facing Arnold, Washington extends his hand toward the advancing major. Benedict recognizes the signal as "Halt," which he does.

Even from his distance, Arnold can make out that Washington appears to be comparing the envelope contents to a chart on his desk, a chart similar to the one that Peggy had used to decipher the message about General Clinton's plan to devalue the Colonial currency.

After Washington finishes reading the note, he waves for the major to approach.

Pointing to the edge of his desk. The general barks at Benedict, "Hand me that calendar."

Benedict hands Washington the calendar and says, "Sir, I—"

"Hush," Washington says. "I'm calculating. Let's see, Mrs. Arnold supplied me this cipher." Washington removes Peggy's note from a desk drawer and shakes it in the air. "This other—this new note—has just arrived by courier."

Washington points to the calendar. "Let's see. Figure this with me, Major. You and the guardsmen took one day to travel to Philadelphia and did not contact the enemy for another three days ... then I saw Lieutenant Anderson a day later ... Anderson's ride from here to Philadelphia took an additional day and you just now another. That makes, let's see ... one ... two, three, four ... five, six, and seven ... seven days since we first learned about Clinton's currency scheme from Peggy's deciphering of her dispatch from the Philadelphia courier."

"Philadelphia courier?"

"Yes, your wife calls him the Philadelphia jockey. At hardly five feet tall, he'd never meet the standards to be a member of my lifeguard, Benedict."

"I meant to mention this earlier, sir, but before I left Philadelphia to serve here, I did arrange for a few connected pseudo-Loyalists there to keep me informed. Over the weeks, Mrs. Arnold has been good enough to have trained them a little, by letter, in a cryptography of sorts—to maintain secure messaging, that is. I hope that that meets with your approval, sir."

"Certainly, Major. Security by all means, especially considering how efficient your Philadelphia spies are compared to our Culpers. For instance, take a look at this." He hands Arnold the note.

Arnold has only time to glance at the note before Washington says, "It's the same damned message, Benedict. Not identical wording, mind you, but it tells the same things regarding Clinton's plan ... a plan about which your Peggy informed us a full seven days ago."

"Sir, was the courier from Connecticut?"

"Yes, yes. And that is what is so troubling. Tallmadge and the whole New York Five are proving to be too damned slow, Major. The slugs are risking their lives to deliver to me news that is one week old. Can you speed them up for me, Benedict?"

"How do you mean, sir?"

"Benedict, I've been thinking ... if you were in charge of my Culper snails, could you prod those Long Islanders into a tempo more akin to that of our Philadelphia sources?"

"Sir, I need not remind you of the differences in the logistics of the two undertakings. Namely that Philadelphia is an appreciably nearer source for our espionage than New York City."

"Quite true, quite true, but I mean to have both cities, and I mean to have you in command of our five New Yorkers and in command of ... however many it is ... of your Philadelphians. You're now in charge of both cities, all of our spies. Do you understand?"

"Yes, sir, and thank you for your trust, but what about my current assignment, Your Excellency's lifeguard.

"Major, you need not be concerned about the lifeguard any longer. I shall turn over that responsibility to Captain Hamilton. As of this minute, Benedict, your only responsibility is our spies. Make that your top priority—your only priority. And feel free to commandeer anything you need, any personnel you require, and let not any expense impede you. Just ask and it is yours."

"Aye, sir."

Washington adds, "And, Major, if you and your wife are able to continue giving me intelligence from your Pennsylvania snoopers days in advance of the intelligence from the Long Island Five, then we need to find whatever means necessary to reward the Philadelphia informants and to encourage your Culpers to be more like your Philadelphians."

"I am your humble servant, Your Excellency."

"Now, lift a pen, Ben. I need you to make a list of the New Yorkers in your Culper gang. You know the roster only partially, but this will be the whole of it."

Benedict acquires paper, pen, and ink from the commander's desk.

Washington asks, "Are you ready?"

Ben nods, and the general recites from memory the names and code names of the Long Islanders: "Agent 721, Major Benjamin Tallmadge (alias John Bolton), Agent 722, Abraham Woodhull (alias Samuel Culper), got that so far?"

"Yes, sir."

Washington continues, "Agent 723, Robert Townsen (alias Samuel Culper Jr.), Agent 724, Austin Roe, and Agent 725, Caleb Brewster. I shall fill you in on other particulars, in due time. Did you get all of those?"

"Yes, sir."

Washington adds, "By the way, which one of your Philadelphia men is this?" The general is looking at Peggy's week-old deciphering. "This ... this ... Agent 711? You know, his role has proven quite invaluable in your recent securing of our nation's currency paper ... come to think of it ... as was his role in our earlier arrest of the guardsman, Hickey, in that kidnapping plot weeks ago. Remember?"

"I remember, and I admire 711's contributions as much as you do, sir. Truth be told, I had taken for granted that he was one of your—one of our—Culper Five.

"He is not one of my Philadelphia spies. I shall inquire of Major Tallmadge in Connecticut as to 711's identity. Perhaps our Culper Ring of Five has become a Culper Ring of Six."

CHAPTER 12
Benedict's Father-in-Law

In Philadelphia, Peggy Arnold's father is still able to mingle with Colonial patriot dignitaries as well as bigwigs among the Loyalists. Judge Shippen's invitees to his South Fourth Street mansion are happy to be in his presence and happier yet to imbibe in the fruits of Shippen's wine cellar.

On this particular day in late June 1779, one invitee just happens to be a second cousin to Peggy's old flame, Colonel John André, now the trusted aide to General Clinton in New York City as Clinton's spymaster. Franklin Muir, from all appearances, seems to be overflowing with the bubbly and belching its residue upon any houseguest within his shadow's length.

Muir manages to draw Judge Shippen aside for a tête-à-tête. He whispers, "You do know, don't you, that I am your most knowledgeable guest at this party?"

Shippen chuckles and says, "Nay, sir. I'll have you know that you are dining here amongst the intelligentsia of this city. What makes you think that—"

"Never you mind, never you mind about that. I tell you that am the most knowledgeable here because I know something that none of your other guests know. They don't know it because they don't have the ear of John André the way I—"

"Colonel John André, you mean?"

"Yes, him, my Cousin John, 'cept he's now General John André. Got a promotion, didn't he? He just happens to be Clinton's right-hand man now, you know ... well, Cousin John has asked me to hand you this note, if I ever

51

was to talk to you in private, that is, this note here." He waves a folded paper. "But it's not for you, Judge. 'Tis a secret. Shh! Shh! It is for John's true love, your daughter Peggy ... for her eyes only, as they say."

"Stop right there, sir. I shall be no party to any correspondence from John André to Peggy or to anyone else in my family."

Muir says, "But ... but if you do not deliver this note, then I shall not be obliged to tell you what it is that I know that makes me the most knowledgeable guest at this party. I shall not tell you what I know—what nobody else here knows—about General Clinton. None of you know where General Clinton is about to attack. I have friends in high places ... I do know."

"Dear Fellow, we all are quite certain that Clinton shall head to Morristown ... Morristown, New Jersey, to take on the commander in chief's encampment."

"Certain are you? That shows how little you know ... I'll tell you, you just don't know a thing. Clinton wants no part of General Washington, not yet, at least. But wait now, before I tell you my inside information, tell me, are you taking John's note for your daughter or not?"

Judge Shippen says, "Give it here, I guess. I suppose that I'll see that my daughter gets it. What's Clinton up to?"

Muir hands over his folded note. "He wants to kill the Frenchies, don't you know?"

"What Frenchies? We have no Frenchies."

"The Frenchies in Rhode Island, I'm talking about—boatloads of 'em."

"You do not mean at Newport, do you?"

"Yep, at Newport, a goodly portion of their fleet ... and, sir, I notice that my glass has gone empty. Have you run out of wine?"

"Here, here, take mine." Shippen hands Muir his glass, which André's cousin eagerly puts to his lips. Judge Shippen adds, "But Clinton has no ships at Newport, does he?"

"That's all right. That's all right. He don't need no ships. He's settin' a land trap for the Frenchie boats. They'll not make it to shore ... hic!"

"What else do you know about Clinton's plan?"

"Nothin', nothin' till you give me your daughter's return message. I have lots more, lots more. And I also can drink me lots more of your fine wine, come to think of it. Do we have a bargain?" As the two men shake hands,

Muir says, "I have friends in high ..." His eyes close, and he slumps to the floor.

Shippen props his drunken guest to a wall, and opens the folded letter addressed to Peggy. Edward Shippen glances at the note and mutters to himself, *André still wants to use numbers instead of words with Peggy, does he?*

Shippen leaves the grand room and heads toward his library desk. The Judge must pen a letter to Peggy regarding his discovery of General Clinton's plan to attack the French fleet.

Perhaps it is the wine or that the judge believes that he has taken too many minutes to finish his correspondence, but, in his haste to leave his desk, he stumbles, landing facedown on the floor, papers strewn about. In seconds, he rights himself and gathers up the sheets.

Usually the epitome of class and grace, Edward uncharacteristically barges at full speed—for a man his age—into his room of guests, hurriedly looks around, and beckons one of the youngest, healthiest servants within sight. Shippen knows that it will require a young man for the hard ride ahead of him.

Edward Shippen accompanies the servant out to the stable.

The young man saddles a steed and mounts.

The judge hands the rider his note and the encrypted message. "Do not stop until you reach my daughter at Morristown. Sleep as little as you must. Use a lantern if you must—and get to Mrs. Arnold with all speed."

As the messenger rides off, Edward thinks, *If the drunken cousin has come around, perhaps I can squeeze some more juicy morsels out of him about his Frenchies. Either way, this is bound to be something Peggy can use.*

CHAPTER 13
Philadelphia Couriers

Shortly after sunrise, Edward Shippen's rider arrives at the Morristown encampment. A slightly built rider had joined him only about a mile or two away from Philadelphia. Both riders approach a guard and stop at his command.

"Messages from Philadelphia," one rider says.

The guard receives two envelopes from one courier and a single envelope from the shorter rider. The guard says, "All correspondence is for Mrs. Arnold?"

One rider says, "Yes, sir."

The other rider nods.

The guard keeps the envelopes, bids farewell to the couriers, and hurriedly walks to the Arnolds' living quarters.

Peggy has just finished a light breakfast.

The guard knocks and waits until Peggy comes to the door. He turns over the three envelopes to Peggy and says, "From Philadelphia, ma'am." The guard scurries back to his post.

Peggy opens all three envelopes, sees that only one is encrypted, and stuffs it into her apron. *I will decipher this one later.*

It takes but a glance at the other two letters for Peggy to recognize the possible military significance of their subject matter. Because her husband has just begun dressing for his morning duties, Peggy decides that she must somehow get these two intelligence communiqués into the hands of General Washington.

Peggy hurries through the mansion to the general's living quarters and encounters the commander in chief's guard. "Is the general awake? Is he at breakfast yet?"

"One might say so, ma'am, but more rightly said, it is the breakfast which is at him. I have delivered it to him from the kitchen tent just a few minutes ago."

"Will you please inquire of His Excellency if I might seek audience with him whilst he is eating? It is an unusual request, I know, but I have messages to deliver of the utmost urgency. And will you please hurry?"

The guard enters Washington's room, is gone but a few seconds, and returns. "His Excellency wishes your immediate presence, Ma'am."

Entering the general's dining room, Peggy finds Washington raising a cup of tea to his lips. "Good morning, sir. I trust that you are enjoying your breakfast." She approaches the general.

"I have enjoyed it, Peggy, but I'm enjoying this fresh brew even more. Won't you join me in a cuppa?"

"Thank you, sir, but no. Instead, I have timely messages that might prove to be of military import to you." She extends the envelopes toward the general.

"No, no, Peggy. Allow me, please, to finish my cup. Please read them to me."

Peggy nods, opens the envelopes, and removes the contents. "Your Excellency, General Clinton will soon march troops to Rhode Island. Sincerely, Judge Edward Shippen, Philadelphia."

Washington looks up from his cup, "From your father?"

She nods.

"And the other note?"

"Sir, General Clinton, within the fortnight, will march cannons and three thousand men nigh on two hundred miles from Newtown, Long Island, to Newport to ambush the French fleet of General Rochambeau. Your loyal servant, Agent 711."

"My God, Peggy! No disrespect intended toward your father, but did you hear the differences between his and Agent 711's letter? The agent's enumeration and other specifics make me wish your father's message had remained in invisible ink."

Peggy whispers, "Sir, neither note used the *medicine*. They—"

"I know, I know ... please forgive my rudeness, Peggy. Both messages are valuable, and your father has done well enough. It's just that one message is a great deal more useful than the other. Forgive my bluntness and please convey my thanks to Judge Shippen ... and to your Agent 711."

"No need to ask forgiveness, sir, and this Agent 711, well, he is not mine, I'm sure."

"Yes, yes, I understand. I shall ask your husband to communicate my gratitude to 711. Speaking of whom, is Benedict about?"

"I shall retrieve him for you and point him in this direction."

"Very good. And in my haste, I fear that I have neglected to also thank you, my lady, for bringing the two messages to my early attention."

"You are quite welcome, Your Excellency." She curtsies and exits.

Soon Peggy's husband arrives at Washington's desk. "Good morning, General. Peggy has informed me about her father's intelligence communiqué."

"Ben, good morning. First things first, Major. First of all, forget everything I said about your having nothing more to do with my bodyguard. I want you to take them—as many as you need and as soon as possible toward New York City—with no waste of time. I'll have Captain Hamilton accompany you with artillery. You are to execute a diversion."

"A diversion, sir?"

"Indeed, I need Clinton to believe that my whole army is attacking him. My plan will require you and your men to be loud, to be seen, but to stay out of harm's way. I must keep Clinton from his planned march to Rhode Island. I need General Rochambeau to land there unimpeded."

"Rochambeau? Newport?"

"Yes, yes, this Agent 711 is telling us—"

"Agent 711? Pardon the interruption, sir."

"Yes, yes. Did Mrs. Arnold not tell you?"

"No, sir, I made double time here as soon as she told me about Judge Shippen's note."

"Well, the important thing is that Clinton wants to march north to intercept the French fleet at Newport. I can't have it. We mightily need the Frenchmen to safely join us on our soil."

"Sir, it occurred to me—might you give me temporary command of part of your infantry in addition to the lifeguard men?"

"What part of it do you mean?"

"Those men, the ones we last paraded here, the ones posing as Indians."

"You mean, our sham five hundred that masqueraded for Clinton's spies?"

"Yes, sir, five hundred should suffice."

"I'll have Hamilton give them the order. I can see where you're going with this, Benedict. It just might work again. We both know that Clinton is already aware of exactly how many soldiers I command. The least that this ruse should do is remind him of our additional five hundred painted savages. But enough talk. Ben, go now to your lifeguard and ready them ... and send Hamilton to me."

Within two hours, Arnold and Hamilton prepare the bodyguard, the cannon wagons, the infantrymen turned Indians, and the food and munitions for the expedition to New York. The small army begins its trek.

Morristown is but a fraction of a day's march from New York City, so Benedict Arnold's diversion against Clinton can begin later that day.

CHAPTER 14
Equine Man's Bluff

After several hours of marching, Arnold's band of soldiers manages to advance to the New Jersey-owned west bank of the Hudson River. Within half a mile of Fort Lee—formerly held by the Colonials—Benedict orders a halt. "Captain Hamilton, place your artillery along this line." He sweeps his hand, pointing to the high ground parallel to the river. "There's no higher ground that I can see, can you?"

"We are only about twenty-five to thirty feet elevated above the water, but I have seen none higher."

"Side by side with those cannons, Alexander, and spaced apart. Do likewise with the men. Have them flank the cannons and spaced sufficiently. We want to allow the enemy to see the breadth of us, but permit him only to surmise about our depth." Hamilton calls out the orders and the guard and wagon drivers begin to place the artillery.

When cannons and men are in position, Hamilton asks, "Major, is the fort not beyond the range of our cannons?"

"Aye, and we should be beyond range of theirs. We wish, Alexander, to feign an assault—and avoid being assaulted. We hope never to need the use of our smaller firearms. Now fix our 'Indians' in place such that they also are easily visible to the enemy."

Hamilton salutes and leaves the major to execute the orders. Minutes later, the captain returns and says, "All done, sir."

"Fire your cannons when ready, Captain."

Alexander Hamilton issues the command, and half the artillery opens

59

fire. After a pause, he calls out again. After the other half of the artillery issues its blasts, Alexander turns to Ben and says, "Just short of the fortification, sir."

"Let's trust that theirs will fall short of us as well. We shall wait."

After five to ten minutes, gray smoke clouds rise above Fort Lee. "Here it comes," Captain Hamilton says. Seconds later, the Americans hear the booming from the British artillery. The enemy's propelled spheres do appreciable damage to trees and soil, but they land well in front of the American line.

"Let's exchange further with them, Alexander—let them know that we are serious."

Captain Hamilton issues the orders, and the Colonialist artillery volleys, pauses, and volleys again. The Americans wait once more. And they wait some more, but the British do not return fire. Hamilton, peering through binoculars, says, "They're sending infantry at us, Major—hundreds."

Benedict says, "We shall fire half of the cannons, but we're going to begin loading the others up to the horses. Alexander, it's time to initiate our tactical withdrawal."

"We are retreating, sir?"

"Aye, but we are leaving sufficient artillery on this ridge for the enemy to think we are still here. Is your horse fast, Alexander?"

"None faster in our entire army, I'd wager. Why do you ask, sir?"

"There is no time to discuss it, but I need you to ride one of my guard's horses instead of your swift one."

"But what about the guardsman?"

"Well, I suppose he must ride one of the wagon horses—from one of the wagons we are leaving behind. I need you to ride the guardsman's horse and bring your fast one by its reins to follow me."

"You are leading the retreat?"

"No, to the contrary, Alexander. You and I will be charging the British infantry."

"But, sir, they are at least hundreds if not a thousand strong."

"Listen, Captain, you and I will be merely feigning a charge—just part of the way toward the fort—and then we shall join the others in the withdrawal."

"But there are only two of us, yet we are taking three horses."

"No time to talk, Alexander. Make the horse swap. I shall explain the rest when we are mounted."

Alexander Hamilton selects a soldier, gives him the order, and mounts the guardsman's relatively slow horse. He grabs the reins of the speedier one and leads it to Arnold.

Benedict says, "On our two-man faked charge, Alexander, at some point, I will be horseless—"

"You think your horse will have an accident, Major?"

"No, Captain. I will intentionally be getting off my horse."

"You'll be on foot, sir?"

"Yes, but only temporarily. If all goes well—and I see no reason why it should not—I shall be remounting, but mounting your fast horse instead of this one."

"But, sir, are we not putting ourselves at risk? Did not General Washington order us to avoid—"

"Rest assured, you will be charging with me only part of the way. You and the spare horse will follow me at a safe distance. I shall be somewhat ahead of you, but not beyond running distance."

"My running distance, sir?"

"Nay, Captain, it is my running distance, my running from my riderless horse, that is, away from the enemy back toward you and toward this extra horse. Then we both shall gallop to join our retreating fellows."

"Sir, I fear that you indeed are putting yourself in harm's way. Would you please reconsider?"

"The enemy is on foot, we shall be as the hare fleeing the tortoise. I promise you. The only small risk is in getting this horse to fall without falling on much of me."

"You shall be felling your horse?"

"No more questions—it's time for our charge. Lieutenant, cease fire. Begin the withdrawal—the same path that brought us here!"

Hamilton shouts out the orders, the cannons quit, the loading for the retreat begins, and Benedict says, "Alexander, give me your sidearm. You shall be beyond the enemy's range, but I might have need for a second weapon."

After Alexander obliges, the two mounted soldiers and their three horses head down the gentle slope toward Fort Lee and toward the enemy infantrymen. After a few hundred yards, Benedict veers off to the left.

61

Alexander says, "Where are we going?"

"We're going to make almost a half circle beginning off here to the left. Follow me," Ben says.

Alexander joins Benedict, and the spare horse trails Hamilton.

In the silence of what is virtually a cease-fire by all parties, Benedict says, "You and I shall be coming into the enemy's field of view from their right side. I wish for it to appear to the enemy infantry that we have unexpectedly crossed their line of march."

Hamilton nods.

The two horsemen have almost completed their clockwise arcing route toward the marching enemy. Benedict and his horse are nearly finished his planned half circle, when he lets out a yell to attract the attention of the British foot soldiers. He succeeds, and the redcoats begin to fire at the two riders.

Arnold says, "Take the lead now, Alexander, but turn your steed toward your mates and away from the British." Captain Hamilton, still on the borrowed horse and still leading his own faster riderless horse by its reins, begins to separate himself from Arnold.

Hamilton arcs away from Benedict, separating them from each other by about ten lengths. The captain points the horse under his saddle and the riderless one back toward the knoll.

Benedict says, "Hold that distance, Alexander, but continue to glance back to check my condition. When you see me on foot, come to a halt. I hope to run up to your position and mount our spare horse."

"Can't quite hear you, sir. Please repeat."

Arnold repeats his instructions, only at a louder volume, and Hamilton says, "Aye, sir."

When Alexander hears a gunshot from not far behind him, he turns in the saddle and sees Arnold's horse in a stumbling gait, favoring its left hind leg, but still at a near gallop.

Moments later, Alexander turns to ascertain Arnold's status when he sees the major fire a pistol shot into his horse's right hind leg.

Benedict's horse suddenly stops in its tracks, its hindquarters collapsing beneath it. Upon his horse's abrupt halt, Arnold is thrown forward through the air. He rolls heels head over heels and comes to a kneeling, forward-inclining stop with his arms stretched out to break his tumble.

Arnold stands, shakes the cobwebs from his head, and sprints toward Hamilton. He stops and mounts the spare horse. He and Alexander look back at the widening distance they are making between themselves and the pursuing enemy. Benedict asks, "Do you have your binoculars?"

"Yes I do." Both riders halt.

"Tell me what the British are doing."

"They have quit, Major. I can see that without the glass. They can never overtake us now, sir."

"Are they doing anything else?"

"Well it looks as if some of them are examining your downed horse. I see smoke and—"

A gun blast interrupts Alexander.

The captain says, "One of the regulars has put your animal out of its misery, I believe. And another, yes, another soldier is opening your saddlebag. What's he doing? Looks like he's removing a white cloth or white paper. Now ... now he's handing it to an older redcoat ... yes, one with a brighter red uniform than the others and with something shiny, perhaps metal, at his neck."

"An officer, I presume ... good, good, I am glad for it."

"If that's an officer, he's turning some of his men around. No, no, all of them are turning around. Appears they're heading back to Fort Lee ... yes, the whole lot."

Satisfied that the enemy has quit the chase, the two officers resume their horseback beeline toward their mates.

When Arnold and Hamilton join the rest of their band, the captain says, "Would you please explain why you chose to take such a risk against the enemy infantry back there?"

Benedict says, "You saw the officer with the white paper, did you not?"

"White cloth or white paper—I could not tell which."

"It was indeed paper—paper on which I had written General Washington's battle plan for his assault upon New York City."

"But ... but General Washington has no battle plan with which to attack New York City. We both know that."

"You know that, I know that, but Clinton and the British do not ... until now."

"But, sir, how did the plan get into your saddlebag, when did—"

"It has been there since early this morning at headquarters when I composed it whilst waiting for you and the lieutenant to prepare our men for this phony attack."

"You composed it? With or without General Washington's order, may I ask?"

"Without it, Captain, without it. 'Tis why I am a major and you are still a captain, Alexander."

"I see the value in getting a false battle plan into the hands of the enemy, I do, but I also see the two risks you have taken."

"Two risks?"

"Aye, in your risking life and limb a moment ago against the enemy's infantry and in risking the same life and limb by usurping your commander in chief's authority."

"Alexander, we shall see. We shall see if I pay for what you deem to be usurpation, or if I am to be paid for a brilliant stratagem. The man you are looking at is Major Arnold, the man you will see when we return to Morristown will be Colonel Arnold. I guarantee it."

"For your sake, Major, I hope that you are right. But be that as it may, will you please tell me the particulars of General Washington's—I mean your—plan of attack?"

"Let me first say that two occurrences here on the Hudson prompted me to follow through in my attempt to allow the false battle plan to fall into the hands of the enemy. First was the failure of our cannons to impress Fort Lee's armed guard at all, and their counterattack proved to be far more legitimate than our feigned one. Those two events confirmed my fears that Clinton would need additional convincing."

"Convincing?"

"In order to persuade him that we are actually about to attack his stronghold here in the city. As for the plan's details, we'll have time for that on our passage back to Morristown."

Arnold's band of guards and pseudo-Indians continue back to Morristown.

* * *

The British infantry officer reads Benedict's fake battle plan. By standard chain of command, he has promoted Arnold's paper from officer to officer until—after the paper has been escorted twelve miles or so—it eventually reaches the British headquarters at Newtown, Long Island.

There, Lieutenant General Henry Carle—second-in-command to General Clinton—rushes to this commander's office.

Clinton calls out an invitation for Carle to enter. "What have you there, Henry?"

"A captured document, sir."

"Captured from whom? How?"

"From the saddlebags of a Colonial messenger—or at least a rebel horseback rider—who was caught in the crossfire between our Fort Lee infantry and an American artillery attack force."

"Fort Lee? Enemy artillery? Why was I not informed of this, Carle?"

"Sir, I just this minute learned of it as well."

"And our fort—do we still have it. And the rebels, where are they? Speak up, man."

"The fort for now is well, but our officers there report enemy artillery on a bluff to the west."

"And the rebel messenger? Dead or alive?"

"Escaped, sir."

"And the captured document?" Clinton nods toward the sheet in Carle's hand. "It looks rather small. Can it be worth our time to study it?"

"Sir, study it is what I have begun. I trust that you will deem it worthy of our attention. Shall I read it to you?"

"The very thing. Get on with it."

General Carle lifts the paper to a reading distance and begins: "The office of commander in chief, Continental Army, dated—"

"Spare me the fool's credentials. I cannot bear to hear such honor heaped upon any of these upstarts ... get to the point, Henry."

Carle continues reading:

1. Gentlemen, we are about to reclaim the Hudson.
2. Immediately divide main army's twenty-eight regiments into four equal quarters.

3. One-quarter to maintain guard over Morristown—Major Arnold in command.
4. The other three-quarters to advance to New York City, one week from today.
5. General Howe's seven regiments to advance to Fort Washington via Shoemaker's Bridge.
6. General Lee's seven regiments to advance to Fort Washington via Flatbush Road.
7. My own seven regiments to advance to Fort Washington via King's Bridge.
8. We meet in counsel to develop detailed strategy tomorrow after morning meal.

General Clinton's countenance reddens as he stands and shouts, "The damned fool! And to top it all, the damned fool is a copycat. He wants to use the same avenues of approach to the fort as we did when we took the fort from him back in '76. Has he no imagination whatsoever? And the ignorant son of a bitch has the gall to still call our Fort Knyphausen by his own name. He dishonors our Hessian comrade who helped take that fort from the rebels in the first place. If he thinks … if Washington thinks he can get his precious fort back into Colonial hands, he has another thing coming. Never! I swear, never! The Hudson is mine."

Carle says, "But he appears quite determined. I mean, he's leaving a mere major—this Major Arnold—in charge at Morristown and sending all of his big-gun generals at us. And it's a significant number of men they plan on sending at us. Let's see … seven … fourteen … twenty-one regiments, sir."

"And what do we know about Washington's number of men in each regiment, Henry?"

"At last report, sir, the Americans have between seven hundred and eight hundred men per regiment. That means as many as, what, about 5,600 attacking by Shoemaker's Bridge, another 5,600 approaching by Flatbush Road, and the same number coming down King's Bridge."

General Clinton smiles and says, "Henry, the capturing of this war plan has been a quite fortunate and timely coup. We shall ditch our planned march to Newport immediately. Scuttle those plans right now. We're going to stay home. That's what we're going to do. Henry, we are going to match—nay, we shall overmatch—Washington's numbers at his three-pronged attacking sites, and we shall reinforce Fort Knyphausen with the cannons that we are no longer taking to Rhode Island. Give the necessary orders to cancel the trek to Newport, Henry. We probably have a week to ready ourselves here for these obstinate, overconfident rebels. We shall show them a welcoming party that they shall not soon forget."

CHAPTER 15
General Washington Debriefs Major Arnold

When Benedict Arnold and his crew return to Morristown, Arnold and Hamilton report immediately to George Washington inside the Ford Mansion. All three officers are seated.

Washington asks, "How went your attack on Fort Lee, Benedict?"

"Very well, I believe. They knew that we meant business. So much so that they returned artillery fire and sent several hundred foot soldiers at us."

"And what action did you take against their infantry?"

"A measured retreat, sir, and they did not follow. I believe they wished to come no nearer to our cannons. We left half of our pieces on a knoll, visible to the enemy through their glass from the fort, and I believe their foot soldiers want no part of our artillery, at least for a while."

"Any casualties on our side?"

"None whatsoever, sir—not a scratch."

Captain Hamilton grins and says, "Except for the death of your horse, Major Arnold, if I may say."

George Washington asks, "You lost your horse to enemy fire?"

"Well, yes and no. They fired the final shot, but I fired the first two."

"You shot your own horse … twice?"

"Aye. You see, he would not go down from my first shot."

"Benedict Arnold, I have business to which I must attend, and I usually have no time for such riddles, but this intrigues me. I must ask the obvious, I suppose. Why did you wish for your horse to go down?"

"I had hoped that the enemy would find my wounded horse and find a paper document in my saddlebag, sir."

"Benedict, you have missed your calling. You shouldn't have been a military officer, but a playwright, a dramatist. The Bard himself would have difficulty matching this tale. So, come now. Come on. Do finish your story."

"The finish has yet to come, sir, and I pray that it be a happy ending. For now, it appears certain that one of their officers has read the sheet."

"Finish! Finish! Finish!"

"You see, sir, the paper the British have read ... well, that paper was your battle plan for your attack upon New York City."

"My what?"

"I took the liberty of fashioning one such attack plan while packing for our feigned assault of Fort Lee."

"You took the liberty to forge a plan under my signature?"

"Forgive my presumptiveness, sir, but I calculated that if our cannons failed to convince the British of our desire to strike their city, then the British would need more convincing. I hoped they would assume the fake battle plan was of your penning."

General Washington says, "Major Arnold, my first inclination for such forgery and usurpation on your part would be a summary demotion in rank for you followed by a court-martial, but having not seen your fictitious plan of assault, I shall temporarily, at least, forego judgment until after hearing the details of just how I should be expected by you to attack New York."

"Begging your pardon, sir, I did not—and would not ever—presume to substitute mine for your strategizing. I merely tried to make the plan believable to the enemy. In fact, I tried to make our fictitious scheme resemble their own successful strategy in taking Fort Washington from us in '76. I hope I made them believe that we were sending twenty-one regiments toward Fort Washington—"

"Twenty-one? I wish to God that I had as many at hand. But if I did, I would happily aim them all at Clinton. And for your sake, Major, I hope to hell that Clinton is not expecting me to aim my few hundreds of regulars at his battery and his impenetrable Fort George."

"No, sir. There are no attacks at Fort George, but at his more vulnerable

Fort Knyphausen—near where we just left some of our artillery planted on high ground."

"Go on, Benedict. What's my strategy supposed to be up there?"

"Well, sir, if all goes well, Clinton will be expecting you to send seven regiments by way of Shoemaker's Bridge, a second seven regiments by way of Flatbush Road, and the final seven regiments—"

"And the final seven regiments by way of King's Bridge?"

"Exactly, and if Clinton remembers how effective those three routes were for the British against us, then he just might be persuaded as to the legitimacy of our plan, which he—I assume and hope—thinks he has managed to capture from us."

General Washington smiles. "Benedict Arnold, your forgery just might prove to have been well worth the trying."

"Perhaps worth a promotion for a certain humble major to the rank of colonel, sir?"

"That remains to be seen, Benedict. You see, your scheme—in theory at least—has a chance for success but an equal chance for failure, I'm afraid.

"Beyond that, I must tell you that I am not pleased with your having abandoned so many of my cannons on the Hudson for the enemy to confiscate. And more importantly, Major, just how and when will we be able to tell if your faked battle plan scheme is working?"

"I shall immediately set our New York spies and Philadelphia spies onto the task, sir, as well as sending a messenger to Rhode Island to ascertain the presence or absence of the British army at or near Newport."

"Fair enough. That might settle the question of your possible promotion, Major. And, by the way, shall spy number 711 be a part of this particular mission?"

"Why do you ask, sir?"

"Well, as you might recall, it was only through Agent 711's note to us in the first place that Clinton's plan to invade Rhode Island was revealed. Without that timely revelation, we would have had no reason to attempt to divert Clinton's attention with your cannon fire on Fort Lee—let alone with your contrived battle plan. Benedict, isn't 711 one of yours in Philadelphia?"

"Well, yes and no. By that, I mean that 711's notes have been from Philadelphia. Perhaps he uses Peggy's father as his contact. I shall inquire about that from my father-in-law."

"By all means, Major, ask Mr. ... uh ..."

"Judge ... Judge Edward Shippen, sir."

"Tell Judge Shippen then that he—and Agent 711—command my greatest esteem."

CHAPTER 16
Independence Day 1779

It is now July 4, 1779. At Morristown, General George Washington has given all enlisted men a day of rest to commemorate the third anniversary of the signing of the Declaration of Independence. The general provides something he had never done before: an all-you-can-eat buffet on his mansion lawn, accompanied by a single glass of ale per attendee. The officers get two glasses.

At the meal's conclusion, they are treated to a modest fireworks display.

Benedict Arnold approaches General Washington. "Thank you, sir, for such a generous and gracious feast and celebration."

"I am only too happy to provide you and the others a diversion from the routine, especially considering the momentous holiday we are celebrating."

"On that subject, sir, the subject of celebrating ... a week from today is my wife's birthday. Peggy loves to dance, and it occurred to me to ask whether it was or was not proper for us to celebrate her birthday with music—that is, music in your mansion headquarters?"

"Benedict, you need not have hesitated in the asking. Your wife—our cryptographer deluxe—deserves at least that much. Her decoding and her Philadelphia connections have been instrumental in some of our most important accomplishments since you two moved to Morristown. Give it no more thought, Benedict. I shall arrange for everything: food, drink, and music. As it happens, I know some musicians among the townspeople—if they can manage on such short notice, and I trust that they will be able to. Peggy's birthday is in seven days?"

"Yes, sir. July 11."

"Consider it done."

CHAPTER 17
Peggy Arnold's Birthday

It is July 11, 1779, at the Continental Army's Morristown encampment. In addition to the local musicians who will be playing for the dance, General Washington has invited Morristown's mayor and his wife and several of the town's other prominent couples to Peggy Arnold's birthday party—as well as about a dozen unmarried females from the community. Because Washington has allowed his officers—those of lieutenant rank and higher—from among his command to attend the party, he has seen the need to supply an adequate number of dance partners for his unmarried officers.

At dusk and just as guests are arriving at Washington's headquarters, a rider approaches the mansion, dismounts, and delivers an envelope to one of the younger officers. The messenger returns to his horse and is gone as the young officer delivers the message to General Washington.

Washington immediately notices that the envelope is addressed to Mrs. Arnold. He joins the couple, draws them off to an alcove away from the crowd, and hands the envelope to Peggy. "This has arrived for you."

"Thank you, sir." She hands the envelope to her husband. "Will you open it for me, Ben?"

Benedict opens the envelope, lifts from it a single, small sheet, and hands it to his wife. "Look, it's encrypted."

Peggy begins to peruse the letter and says, "After the party, I'll sort this out at our quarters."

"But it is so short that you might be able to decipher it now," Benedict says.

"Well, my sweet, it's just that I'd prefer to examine it at my leisure. I'll have time after—"

George Washington says, "If you do not mind, Peggy, I too would like to know the contents of this message—any message sent into my headquarters, for that matter. Should it not take the army's best cryptographer but a moment to decipher such a brief note? Please take a moment, now, if you don't mind." He smiles at Peggy.

"As you please, Your Excellency." Peggy begins to study the single ciphered sentence. The two gentlemen stand quietly as Peggy, from memory and from recent practice, breaks down the ten words. "It's merely a personal birthday message, nothing more. Are we dining soon, sir?"

Ben says, "For heaven's sake, Peggy. It's less than a dozen words. Read it to us."

General Washington nods.

Peggy looks at her note. "My dear Peggy ... please forgive this belated happy birthday wish."

General Washington says, "Signed?"

"No signature," Peggy answers.

General Washington surveys the grand room and waves to the young officer who handed him the note. When he arrives, the general points to the envelope in Peggy's hand. "Who was the messenger who delivered this envelope to you, sir?"

"I know not his name, sir, but he is one of the regular horsemen who brings us correspondence from Philadelphia."

"Can you bring him to me now?"

"I'm afraid not, sir. He left us almost as soon as he came to us."

"Headed in the direction of Philadelphia?"

"Yes, sir."

"Thank you. You may rejoin your friends." He turned to the Arnolds. "What do you make of this?"

Benedict says, "We usually receive messages signed by Agent 711 from Philadelphia. I don't know who else—"

Peggy says, "It must be from my family, perhaps from Father. Precious few people there are even aware that I am alive or aware of my location—let alone aware of the date of my birthday."

Benedict says "But, the note is encrypted. Your father has never before sent ciphered messages."

"He has shown only little interest in my cryptography in the past ... only a little curiosity. Perhaps his curiosity has grown."

"Find the answer to this, Ben. We no longer can be kept in the dark about this 711 fellow. Contact Judge Shippen. Solve this once and for all."

"Yes, sir. And when I discover Agent 711's identity, might you then not consider my promotion to be in order—the promotion which we have discussed before?"

"I cannot guarantee such a thing, Major Arnold. All that I am asking of you is to find out that which you should already have found out months ago. But what I can guarantee you is that if you remain unable to tell me 711's name, then it shall be not a promotion, but a demotion that I shall most likely be considering. A commander in chief cannot have spies who are unknown to him."

"Understood, sir."

The evening's dining commences, followed by the grand room's music and dancing, which brings to a close Peggy Arnold's celebration of her nineteenth birthday.

CHAPTER 18
General Washington Meets General Rochambeau

On September 22, 1880, the general summons Major Arnold to his desk.

Arnold arrives, salutes, greets Washington, and is seated.

"Benedict, I need to communicate with the French at Newport because I seek to confer with General Rochambeau. I am therefore instructing you to correspond with him—through your intelligence chain, if you must. He and I need to meet at some mutually agreeable site to finalize battle plans. Can you arrange it?"

"As soon as possible, sir."

"And try this. Ask him if New London, Connecticut, might not be too far for him to travel from Rhode Island to meet with me."

"I'll start the process immediately."

"When should I expect Rochambeau's reply, Benedict?"

Benedict says, "I'll send a courier now to Agent 721."

General Washington frowns.

Benedict says, "Sir, you know him, Major Benjamin Tallmadge, at Fairfield. I'll instruct Major Tallmadge to take it from there."

"And the time involved for Tallmadge's route?"

"I assume the usual seven to fourteen days, considering the somewhat greater distance to Rhode Island, sir."

"I suppose that it shall be soon enough. I'll leave you to it then."

* * *

79

On October 1, a Philadelphia courier delivers an envelope to a guard at the Morristown encampment's perimeter. After just a brief visit to the camp's mess and an equally brief watering of his horse, the messenger turns his steed back toward Pennsylvania.

The guard hands the message over to the first officer he encounters. "Message from Philadelphia."

The officer delivers the envelope to Captain Hamilton. "From Philadelphia, sir."

Hamilton opens the envelope and examines the message.

George Washington asks, "What is it, Captain?"

"It's encrypted, and it's not a one- or two-line note, sir."

"Where is Major Arnold or his wife? Have you seen either of them today?"

"Mrs. Arnold was at her desk moments ago, sir. Shall I fetch her?"

"Better still, take the note straight to her. Have her report to me at my desk once her deciphering is done. Can you please hurry? And while you're about it, will you find Major Arnold and send him to me."

"Yes, sir."

Hamilton departs, and General Washington heads toward his office.

Minutes later, with the encrypted note in one hand and a second sheet in the other, Peggy Arnold arrives at the commander in chief's desk.

"Please have a chair, Peggy. What have we got?"

Mrs. Arnold hands the encrypted note to the general, keeps the other paper, and sits. "My rushed scribble is unduly illegible, I'm afraid. Captain Hamilton insisted upon my hurried work. May I read it to you?"

"Certainly, and thank you for immediately attending to it."

> Clinton has discovered your intention to rendezvous with Rochambeau at New London. He is sending thousands there by land and sea to ambush what he believes to be but a small contingency escorting Your Excellency to that coastal town. 'Tis not a simple ambush of battle, I fear, but an ambush of assassination. For Clinton has placed a

twenty thousand-pound bounty on Your Excellency's head. Humbly urge cancellation of conference or alternate site.

Your humble servant,
711

Peggy hands the deciphering to Washington.

General Washington stands and eyes the calendar on his desk.

Benedict Arnold walks into the office.

General Washington says, "Benedict, it's been over a week since your Culper gentlemen were assigned the round-trip mission between here and Rhode Island. Do we have any word from them?"

"None yet, sir."

"None yet? None yet! Here, look at this." George's face turns red, and he grabs the sheet from Peggy's hand. "Here is what I've been expecting of you, Benedict. Here is a warning from Philadelphia regarding New London from Agent 711—someone whose name you have never disclosed to me. You haven't discovered 711's identity as yet, have you?"

"Not yet, sir."

"Not yet? Not yet! Is that your only answer to all of this? Can't I expect better from a major who thinks he should be a colonel?"

Benedict opens his mouth to speak, but George Washington says, "Don't answer that. I'll answer it for you. I should expect better. I do expect better!"

"But, sir—"

"Silence!" Washington's face turns even redder. "You listen to this, Benedict Arnold, and you listen well. Whoever this 711 is, it is he who should be promoted, not you. This message ... this message ... see for yourself how 711 has outdone you." He hands Arnold the missive.

Benedict takes the sheet, reads it, and says, "Do you wish me to comment, sir?"

"What I wish ... what I wish is for you to get a new note to Rochambeau for me—and this time, a secure one and not through this damned worthless Culper network. Find this 711, Major, or for God's sake, at least find a way of messaging Rochambeau through him.

"Cancel my conference with the French at New London and find an alternate meeting place—somewhere farther inland, away from Clinton's navy. And on this trip of mine to Rhode Island, you shall be accompanying me with Hamilton and my guard. And if you have any more failures of this nature, you'll become my point scout on that march north. Any assassination fire—and you shall take the first of it. Understood?"

"On top of it, sir."

"And on top of it you had better be, Major."

Benedict and Peggy Arnold exit the general's office. As they navigate the hallways toward their quarters, Ben says, "I would rather that Clinton did assassinate the old fool!"

"Sh! Sh, Benedict! The walls have ears."

"For hell's sake, Peggy. I'd gladly pull the trigger myself."

"Benedict, dear, not so loud."

"I tell you, Peggy, we are on the losing end of this war. You know that, I know that, and thousands of Loyalists in this country know it."

"Ben, your talk about assassination and His Excellency and pulling the trigger yourself are troubling. You must stop. I certainly agree with you that the Loyalists in our midst just might be on the correct side in this war. Father has written to me and said as much about the Tories in Philadelphia."

"And the senile son of a bitch is never going to promote me. I'd be better off with him in the grave. I'd do it myself for half the bounty."

"Benedict, enough! I'm not saying, dear, that ten thousand pounds wouldn't be nice, but calm yourself. For now, put your mind to the task you have been assigned—like you always do."

After a moment of silence and contemplation, Arnold says, "You're right, of course, as usual. Uh … and what was my task, again?"

"Agent 711, you need—"

"I know. I know. I need to discover the identity of this Philadelphia Agent 711, whoever the hell he is. And regarding that city, why has your father not answered us about 711's identity?"

"I am uncertain. We surely have made enough requests of him. Perhaps, whilst you are trekking toward Rhode Island, I might pay Father a visit to learn all we want to know about Agent 711. Although Father has not yet answered our inquiries, I am certain that he can—and will—help us."

"That's just the ticket, Peggy. I'm tired of Old George blaming me for this war that we are losing. In fact, the sooner you can pack and be off to your father's, the better chance I shall have of redeeming myself. When can you leave for Philadelphia?

"I suppose, if need be, I should be able to pack up this evening before bedtime. Can you arrange for an escort for tomorrow morning?"

"That shall be no problem. I'll leave you to your packing then."

CHAPTER 19
Peggy Goes to Philadelphia

In the morning, Peggy Arnold, her small guard detail, and a large quantity of luggage head toward Pennsylvania.

When they arrive at her father's mansion on South Fourth Street that evening, Peggy says, "I'm weary from the day's journey, Father. May I retire and postpone our discussion till morning?"

"Certainly, my dear. And there is surely much for us to discuss."

CHAPTER 20

A Message from Philadelphia

Two days later, a message from Philadelphia arrives at General Washington's Morristown headquarters. The envelope makes its way from guard to lieutenant to Captain Alexander Hamilton.

Hamilton deciphers the message and reports to General Washington.

The general says, "What have we here?"

Hamilton says, "A message I just worked through, sir. It's a bit of trouble, I'm afraid."

"Trouble? Do you mean that was difficult to decipher?"

"I've already done that, sir. It's the content that's so troubling."

"Well, unburden yourself, man. Read it to me."

Hamilton clears his throat.

> Your Excellency ... Beware the Ides of October ... Beware the 20,000 pound bounty ... Beware the major ... Beware the major's desk ...
>
> Your Humble Servant,
> 711

Hamilton says, "Sir, isn't 711 the Philadelphian who cautioned us about the ambush?"

"The one, the very same 711 who warned us of the Brits' kidnapping plot, their counterfeit currency scheme, and their plan to intercept the French fleet at Newport. You know, I have grown to value this invisible Agent 711 more than most of the apparent trustees surrounding me—present company excluded, of course, Captain."

Hamilton says, "But, sir, the Ides?"

"The fifteenth ... the fifteenth of this month, you see."

"And the twenty thousand pounds?"

"The price put on my head by Clinton."

"But which major? What major can this message mean, sir?"

"I have dozens of majors, Alexander. You know that."

"But a major having a desk, sir?"

Washington says, "As far as I know, I have only a single major who has a desk of his own."

"But the message couldn't mean our Benedict, could it, sir? Could it mean Major Arnold?"

"We shall see. We'll just have to ask him about this. Will you fetch him here?"

"I can, but he is presently in the field—overseeing a sidearms target practice of your guards."

"Sidearms? Could you not have done that drill yourself?"

"Yes, sir, but it seems to be one of Benedict's specialties. It's one of his favorites—so he insisted."

"Well, then, you and I must see about his desk. Come with me."

As the two officers walk to Benedict and Peggy's quarters, the general asks, "Is it not too early in the morning to be barging in on Mrs. Arnold?"

"Sir, Mrs. Arnold is on a visit to her father in Philadelphia."

"Of course, of course. When shall she be returning?"

"That I have not heard, sir."

As they arrive at Benedict Arnold's desk, the general says, "Well, his work area seems empty."

"Possibly because we have had nothing at headquarters wanting deciphering until today ... and possibly because Benedict has been out with my guard so much as of late."

"Supervising target practice, you said."

"More than supervising—he gets right down with the men, doing his own practice the last few times."

"Alexander, take a look into his desk drawers if you would."

Captain Hamilton opens all the desk drawers, removes their contents, and places them on the desk."

George Washington counts six box-lock pistols and ammunition among the several crumpled paper sheets on the desk.

The captain lifts one of the pistols and says, "The very type of gun that Benedict has been taking with him to the firing range."

George Washington lifts one of the pistols. "But these pistols have no sights. Their barrels are short—hardly wanting long-range target practice. Is Benedict expecting some sort of close-range duel with General Clinton, do you think?

Hamilton says, "Should I return them to the drawers, sir?"

"Yes, and while you're at it, let's have a look at those papers."

Hamilton puts the pistols back where they came from, flattens several wrinkled sheets, and examines them.

"Well, what has our major been reading?"

"Sir, they are all blank—save for this one."

"Read it for me, Captain."

"Sir, it's encrypted."

"So, decipher it, man. Earn your pay."

Hamilton, out of practice at deciphering ever since the assumption of those duties by Peggy Arnold, sits at Major Arnold's desk for several minutes to finish the deciphering.

Washington paces the floor.

"I'm done," Hamilton says.

"Out with it then. I'm all ears."

Alexander Hamilton reads it aloud.

My dear Major Arnold,

According to the terms of your bargain with General Clinton, he has agreed to convey to you half of the bounty he has offered to his own army. The notes, valued at ten thousand pounds sterling, shall be transferred to you as per your wishes, or to your wife or other heirs in case of your demise—this all in exchange for your successful assassination

89

of the seditious and heretical General George Washington and, of course, our verification of this villain's just deserts. Be assured that all pertinent officers in the king's forces have been alerted to receive you under white flag at a destination of your choosing so as to escort you to safe haven and to the welcoming arms of your British brethren. May your aim be sharp and your horse fleet afoot. Godspeed.

His Majesty's humble servant, General John André, Broadway Barracks

General Washington, jaw unhinged and mouth agape, shouts, "Arnold has betrayed me! Whom can we trust now?" After a quiet pause, the general says, "You know, Alexander, a bit of me, of course, is startled by this revelation, but a larger part of me is saddened. It pains me to think that I am to be betrayed by a trusted comrade—a confidant who shares my mansion with me. It indeed plants a thorn in my heart. And—adding insult to injury—is this half-bounty thing. Arnold is settling for half of the twenty thousand pounds that Clinton is offering his own regulars to kill me. Is my head not worth more to one of my own officers than it is to a common enemy soldier? Arnold shall answer for that and answer dearly."

Hamilton remains silent.

Washington says, "And did you hear the words, Captain? The 'welcoming arms of his British brethren.' Well, we shall see if his British brethren can save him now." Washington grabs Alexander by his shoulders. "Captain, I hereby authorize you to immediately take over Benedict's role of spymaster for us and further authorize you to arrest this treasonous Arnold at once. Take whatever guard you deem necessary and put him in irons. I swear, Alexander, that Arnold has had his last target practice. And I promise that the next gunfire he shall hear shall be that of a firing squad."

CHAPTER 21
Court-Martial

It does not take long for General Washington to assemble a board of senior officers to investigate Major Arnold's suspected treasonous behavior. The board includes General Nathanael Greene (the presiding officer) and Generals Stirling, St. Clair, Lafayette, Howe, Steuben, Parsons, Clinton, Knox, Glover, Paterson, Hand, Huntington, and Stark.

From behind bars, Benedict Arnold continuously and vehemently protests his confinement, loudly proclaiming his innocence.

As Washington is walking within earshot of Arnold's cell window, the major shouts, "If Your Excellency thinks me criminal, for heaven's sake, let me be immediately tried and, if found guilty executed … I ask only justice."

Washington, without missing a step, calls back toward the cell window. "And justice is what you shall certainly be getting, Major Arnold."

General Washington's board of inquiry eventually concludes its pretrial investigation, accumulating evidence sufficient to proceed to Arnold's court-martial hearing.

The general court-martial convenes on October 19 in the grand room of Morristown's Ford Mansion. The judge advocate, John Laurance, begins the session by reading a roll call of the names of the officers on the trial panel.

Major Arnold is standing at attention before the court.

The judge advocate says, "Does the defendant have objection of any member of the court?"

91

Arnold says, "No, sir. I admire and respect the court's membership—both collectively and individually."

Laurance reads the charges against the defendant:

> The defendant, Major Benedict Arnold of the United States Continental Army, is charged with treasonous conduct, to wit, in plotting to aid and assist the Kingdom of Great Britain, an enemy of the United States of America. We allege that Major Arnold conspired with said enemy, with malice aforethought, and for monetary compensation, in a scheme to assassinate an officer of the Continental Army, namely, the commander in chief, General George Washington.

The court president, General Greene, says, "How does the defendant plead to the charges against him?"

"Not guilty, sir," Arnold says.

Greene directs the judge advocate to proceed with evidence for the prosecution.

Laurance says, "If it please the court, I would request permission to read to the court the letter addressed to it from His Excellency, General George Washington."

Greene says, "So granted."

> Gentlemen, Major Benedict Arnold of the United States Continental Army will be brought before you for your examination. Evidence will show that Major Arnold has been in communication with our revolution's enemy, the Kingdom of Great Britain. Said correspondence has placed Major Arnold as the prime mover in a treacherous conspiracy to assassinate an officer of the United States Continental Army, namely, yours truly. Although not all of Arnold's motives are clear, it does appear that monetary gain was prime among them. My representative, Captain

Alexander Hamilton, will provide your honorable panel with particulars of Arnold's treasonous crime.

Your obedient servant,
George Washington

"Proceed with your evidence, Mr. Laurance," announces President Greene.

"If it please the court, we have asked Captain Alexander Hamilton to testify regarding the evidence to which General Washington's letter refers."

General Greene nods.

Alexander Hamilton stands.

Laurance faces Captain Hamilton, swears him in, and says, "What evidence do you deliver to this court?"

"I have this letter from an officer of the enemy addressed to the defendant." Hamilton holds the sheet aloft for the panel. "May I read from it, sir?"

President Greene nods.

My dear Major Arnold,

According to the terms of your bargain with General Clinton, he has agreed to convey to you half of the bounty he has offered to his own army. The notes, valued at ten thousand pounds sterling, shall be transferred to you as per your wishes, or to your wife or other heirs in case of your demise—this all in exchange for your successful assassination of the seditious and heretical General George Washington and, of course, our verification of this villain's just deserts. Be assured that all pertinent officers in the king's forces have been alerted to receive you under white flag at a destination of your choosing so as to escort you to safe haven and to the welcoming arms of your British brethren. May your aim be sharp and your horse fleet afoot. Godspeed.

His Majesty's humble servant, General John André,—"

Laurance says, "I must stop you there, Captain, to ask you to identify for the court the writer of this letter, John André."

93

"Sir, General John André is British General Clinton's chief officer of intelligence."

"And General Clinton would hold André in a position of trust?"

"Yes, sir. Clinton calls André his *spymaster.*"

"So, André would be in a position to be aware of an assassination conspiracy of Clinton's?"

"Yes, André would not only have been aware of it, but more than likely, he was involved in it."

"And how do you know that?"

"Because we have solid grounds to believe that André was involved in previous Clinton schemes against us, sir."

"And those schemes were?"

Captain Hamilton glances at his notes. "In chronologic order, sir, we have no cause to doubt that André was instrumental in (1) the British plot to kidnap His Excellency, (2) their plan to deflate our currency, (3) their plan to intercept French general Rochambeau's fleet at Newport, Rhode Island, and (4) their plan to ambush His Excellency at his conference with Rochambeau at New London, Connecticut."

"And André would have authority to communicate with a member of the Continental Army, to convey Clinton's offer to Arnold of the ten thousand-pound bounty?"

"Yes, sir. Clinton might call André his spymaster, but we commonly refer to André as 'Clinton's right arm.'"

"Will you describe for the court the conditions under which you came to possess this letter from the enemy's General André to Major Arnold."

"It was on this October 4 when General Washington and I discovered the letter from John André inside a desk drawer."

"And to whom did the desk belong?"

"To Major Arnold."

"Did you or General Washington uncover anything else of significance in Major Arnold's desk? And if so, will you describe such?"

"We did indeed. A total of six box-lock pistols and ammunition."

"What, if any, significance do you place to this sort of weaponry?"

Hamilton holds one of the pistols in the air. "It's a type of weapon that can be concealed beneath a soldier's uniform." Hamilton slides the pistol between two undone buttons of his waistcoat.

"Concealment conducive to assassination, perhaps?"

"Perhaps."

"Do the pistols have any other significant bearing upon this case?"

"Yes, sir. It's the type of pistol the major had of late been using in his target practice."

"Possibly practicing, so as to permit Arnold the sharp aim of an assassin as John André's letter encourages him to have?"

"Possibly, sir, and the major is still in possession of my speedy steed, which he never returned to me after Fort Lee."

"The fleet horse—as advised by André?"

"It is one of that kind, yes."

"And would the major daily—or even in the line of his typical duties—be in need of a sharp aim and a fast horse?"

"No, sir. He is General Washington's spymaster. He is not a cavalryman or infantryman."

"Would an assassin profit from the sharp aim and fast horse recommended by André to Arnold?"

"Yes, sir. Of course."

"First, possibly for his completion of the deed and then possibly for his escape?"

"I suppose."

"Perhaps an escape to the 'safe haven and to the welcoming arms' of his 'British brethren'?"

"That could well be."

"And a possible escape to the ten thousand pounds sterling assassination reward."

"So the letter from John André asserts, sir."

The judge advocate faces Major Arnold. "Does the defendant have any questions for this witness?"

The major jumps from his seat and barks, "Captain, you are a liar! You have lied to this panel! Under oath, you have—"

General Greene hammers his gavel again and again. "Order! Order! Major Arnold, you will conduct yourself before this court as an officer of the Continental Army." He shakes an index finger at Benedict. "This panel—not you, sir—shall decide what evidence is a lie and what evidence is the truth. Do you understand me?"

"I beg the pardon of this honorable court, sir. Please forgive me."

Greene nods.

Benedict asks, "May I continue?"

Greene nods again. "With civility this time."

Benedict says, "With all due respect, Captain, the supposed letter from John André that you have read aloud can be nothing but a forgery, as are all allegations here against me equally as fraudulent. I further charge your testimony, in particular, to be illegitimate and unfounded as I shall now demonstrate. For instance, Captain, have you found the supposed remuneration—the ten thousand pounds sterling—to be in my possession?"

"No, sir."

"Therefore, there is no foundation to that claim. I have not been compensated for this hypothetical crime that you have invented."

"No more or no less than any other British soldier could not have collected the assassination bounty payment until after the crime, of course."

"Captain, you mistakenly just now compared me to any 'other' British soldier. I take offense at that slander."

"What you deem slander, sir, others deem reality."

Arnold, face reddening and voice reaching crescendo, points at Hamilton. "Were I not in shackles, sir, I'd be demanding satisfaction—with whatever weapon you should choose. I'd—"

"I'd certainly not choose the box-lock pistols with which you obviously have been rehearsing your assassinating of our commander in—"

"Silence!" General Greene shouts. "The both of you. You will keep this a civil hearing, do you understand?"

Hamilton and Arnold both nod.

Greene says, "The defendant may resume his questioning of the captain."

"All right, all right, then. Let me get back to further proof, Captain, proof that your so-called evidence that you bring to this court if ill-founded, namely the forgery, the fictitious letter that you claim came to me from General John André. My question to you, Captain Hamilton, is how is the court to verify your—erroneous, by the way—contention that the letter you read is actually from General André and not from some pretender?"

"As it happens, sir, with counsel and with panel's permission I have been granted the privilege of returning any question of yours with my own. Therefore I shall now ask you the following. As our army's commanding espionage officer, in charge of all of our intelligence gathering, can you tell this court the location of the British garrison in New York City?"

"Of course, it is Fort George."

"Let me ask you further to specify the location of said fort."

"We, and they, refer to it as the *battery*."

"I shall refrain from asking you to distinguish *we* from *they*—fearing that a turncoat might have difficulties in identifying one from the other."

Arnold looks at the panel of judges and says, "Might I object, sirs, to this additional slander?"

General Greene says, "Captain Hamilton, I concur with the defendant. You have been advised to maintain civility. Therefore, please cease and desist with the epithetical. You have been granted permission to question the defendant—not to make catty remarks. Am I clear?"

"Yes, sir. I beg the court's pardon."

"Continue with your questioning, Mr. Hamilton."

"Major Arnold, the court should find it more of interest if you, with the benefit of your intelligence gathering, are aware of an address for Fort George, specifically a street address."

"Street address?"

"Certainly. You do know what a street is, do you not? The definition of a street is—"

"Captain!" General Greene shouts.

"Sorry, sir," responds Hamilton. "It shall not happen again."

"See that it doesn't. You may proceed with your questions, but only if you mind your tongue."

Hamilton nods and says, "What is the British battery's street address?"

"Street address ... let me think on that ... no ... I think not, Fort George—and battery, of course—that is the extent of our knowledge of the garrison's address."

"Do you know of anyone in the entire Continental Army who does know Fort George's street address?"

"I certainly know not each member of the Continental Army, dear fellow, but no, I have not heard Fort George's street ever named."

"Would it surprise you to learn that the actual address is a street that the British call Broadway, that the Old Dutch formerly called Breed-weg?"

"Both would surprise me, I'm sure."

"Do you expect that members of the British army in New York might well know their own fort's address?"

"I am inclined to agree with that assumption."

"Would you include British officers among those who might know the specifics of the battery's location?

"Of course they must know it … but, sir, I am truly growing weary of this geography lecture."

"Weary you might get, but it so happens that with the court's approval, we have intentionally withheld the final two words from General André's letter to you."

"*Supposed* … supposed letter to me, may I remind the court."

Hamilton again waves the paper sheet above his head. "In this letter, its author pens his signature as follows: 'His Majesty's Humble Servant, General John André … Broadway Barracks.'"

Amid a few audible gasps among the panel of generals, Arnold says, "But how can you—how can any of us—be certain that the address that you have read is reliable?"

"As certain as we are that your network of spies is reliable, for it is they, particularly the most reliable ones in Philadelphia, who have most recently verified for us the Broadway location of General John André. Would you please explain how it is that the writer of this letter I'm holding knows his own true location, but that nobody on our side of this war has known it until now."

Arnold is silent for as long as it takes London's Big Ben to gong out six bells.

Captain Hamilton says, "No, sir. You cannot explain it—and neither can the court explain the authorship of the letter to be other than the name that the author ascribes unto himself and pens it, to wit: General John André."

General Greene says, "Captain Hamilton, do you have any further questions for the defendant?"

"No, sir."

Greene says, "Does the defendant have further questions at this point?"

Arnold remains silent.

General Greene directs the judge advocate to resume his interrogation.

John Laurance says, "Captain, do you have further evidentiary light to shed upon the guilt or innocence of Colonel Arnold?"

"Yes, sir," Hamilton says. "May I elaborate?"

Laurance nods.

Hamilton says, "On the first of this month, the day that we learned about General Clinton's twenty thousand-pound bounty having been placed on General Washington's head, I overheard, right here in the hallways of this mansion, Major Arnold in a loud conversation with his wife regarding the assassination bounty."

"Are there details about that conversation that you can recall?"

"Better still, on that date, I immediately penned what I heard into my daily log for future reference." Hamilton removes his logbook from a valise to display to the court.

Laurance nods. "If you would, please read for the court from your log as to Major Arnold's remarks about the twenty thousand-pound bounty on His Excellency's life."

"With the court's permission, I shall skip the incidentals of the conversation between husband and wife and concisely quote the major."

General Greene says, "You have such permission. You may proceed with your reading."

"These are Major Arnold's words." Hamilton then reads aloud:

> I would rather that Clinton did assassinate the old fool. For hell's sake, Peggy, I'd gladly pull the trigger myself ... we are on the losing end of this war ... and the senile son of a bitch is never going to promote me. I'd be better off with him in the grave. I'd do it myself for half the bounty.

Laurance points at Arnold and says, "So we see here, gentlemen, the defendant—who is not a loyal member of General Washington's inner circle but who is the reincarnation of Judas Iscariot. This modern Judas before you is guilty of sedition, guilty of collaboration with the enemy, guilty of betraying his leader, and in Benedict Arnold's case, betrayal for a bounty but half the thirty pieces of silver."

Another silence fills the room—save for the gasps and whispers among the panel of generals.

The judge advocate says, "Did you or did you not utter these threats?"

Arnold whispers, "But ... but it was a moment filled with anger and frustration. I only ... I only—"

"Never mind that, sir. Just tell this court—did you utter those words?"

Benedict Arnold allows his head to sag, and his chin nearly touches his chest.

After several seconds, Laurance says, "Do you, Major, have a case to present to this court in your defense?"

His chin inching even lower to his chest, Arnold remains silent.

Laurence says, "Sirs, the prosecution rests."

CHAPTER 22
The Court-Martial Panel Reconvenes

One week later, on October 26, at the Ford Mansion, the general court-martial panel reconvenes to announce its decision on the guilt or innocence of Colonel Benedict Arnold. Judge advocate Laurance reads a roll call, and all principles are present.

Court president General Greene asks the defendant to stand before the court and says, "Major Arnold, the court will give you one last opportunity to speak regarding the evidence against you in the conspiracy to assassinate General George Washington. You may discuss your alleged language about our losing this war, language about your failure to gain promotion in office, or whatever else you so desire."

Benedict says, "Sirs, as for winning or losing the war, let me just say that I am impressed that the mass of the people are heartily tired of the war. And all I can say concerning General Washington's failure to promote me from major to colonel and his failure to reward me for my past service is that I daily discover so much ingratitude among mankind that I almost blush to be of the same species."

General Greene says, "Major Arnold, it is the unanimous decision of this court that you are guilty as charged of treasonous conduct in the aiding and the abetting of the Kingdom of Great Britain, enemy of the United States of America. It is the particular judgment of this court that the defendant is guilty of planning, in conjunction with said enemy, the assassination the Continental Army's commander in chief, General George Washington."

The courtroom is quiet.

General Greene says "Colonel Arnold, it is the further decision of this court that the defendant shall be sentenced to death by hanging ... one month from this date."

After a few quiet seconds, Arnold says, "My dear sirs, may I humbly beseech you to rethink the sentencing. I humbly request Your Honors to make but a single adjustment, that of allowing me the honor of a military firing squad—befitting a long-standing military officer in the Continental Army, or in any army, for that matter."

President Greene says, "The court, having anticipated such a request from the defendant, has consulted with His Excellency regarding alteration of sentence from death by hanging to death by firing squad. General Washington concurs with this court that he who has been convicted of high treason deserves not the more honorable execution, but the more ignominious death. Defendant's request is denied."

General Greene, banging the gavel, says, "This case is closed."

CHAPTER 23
Benedict's Fate

On November 26, 1780, hundreds of Morristown townspeople have come to the Ford Mansion's front lawn and roadway as spectators. Every officer of Arnold's court-martial panel and all the soldiers under General Washington's command at the Morristown encampment are in attendance.

The gallows is simple: a horse, wagon, a driver, and a rope appended to a sturdy, overhanging branch of one of the white oak trees that line the roadway.

Bedecked in his finest officer's dress uniform and polished boots, Arnold, two guards, and General Greene have climbed onto the wagon's flat floor.

General Greene begins to place the noose around Arnold's neck.

Benedict says, "Will you allow me? Will you unbind me?"

The general nods, and one of the guards unties the rope from Arnold's hands.

Greene hands the noose to Arnold, who lifts the rope and lowers it upon his neck, cinching it firmly in place.

The general says, "Major, you have an opportunity to speak if you desire."

Benedict, scanning the audience as if beseeching one and all, loud and clearly asks, "I pray you to bear me witness that I meet my fate like a brave man."

General Greene asks, "Are you done?"

"Aye, sir."

Greene lifts a white handkerchief toward Arnold's face, but Benedict's left hand intercepts that movement. "General, will you grant me the opportunity to undergo this punishment without blindfold, and might I not be allowed to hold the handkerchief and drop it as the signal to your driver?"

General Greene asks, "And shall you drop it soon?"

"Immediately, sir."

"Then yes, on condition that there is no dropping of it until the guards and I have descended to the ground. Is that agreed?"

"Indeed. I shall await your descent."

As the two guards and General Greene climb down from the wagon to stand among the spectators, Benedict searches the faces of the crowd. Not finding his wife among them, he wonders, *And where is my dear Peggy?*

The crowd's wait is about to end. Benedict raises the blindfold aloft, pauses a second, and releases the handkerchief. Like a feather in breezeless air, it wafts its way toward the ground.

The wagon driver, chin turned onto his shoulder to observe the prisoner behind him, notices the falling cloth and snaps his whip above his horse's ear. As the horse begins its gallop, the wagon pulls from beneath the feet of Benedict. His body lunges down a few inches until the rope's tightening noose jerks Benedict's body back skyward those same few inches.

The audible cracking sound emanating from the prisoner's cervix tells all witnesses near the gallows that the Continental Army's major Benedict Arnold has breathed his last.

CHAPTER 24
The Widow, Mrs. Peggy Arnold

During Benedict's November 26 execution, Peggy Arnold has remained at her father's house in Philadelphia. Although Ben had written to her about his plight from his cell, he had received no answer from her.

On the morning of November 28, a message from Morristown arrives at the Shippen's South Fourth Street mansion. Judge Edward Shippen opens the envelope, reads the note, and calls for his daughter. When Peggy joins her father, Edward says, "Peggy, Benedict is dead."

"Has he been buried?"

"Not yet. But the time has come. The time is ripe for you to add the last straw to the sheaf. Have you packed?"

"Packed and ready. Have you made the arrangements?"

"Your carriage awaits. I need only call upon your driver."

"And my pass?"

"Right here, my darling." Judge Shippen removes a sealed envelope from one of his pockets and hands it to Peggy. "Put it in a safe place."

Peggy stuffs the envelope down the inside front of her blouse. "I'll keep it close to my heart."

"All right then. I'll have my man take your luggage to the carriage. I'll instruct him to fetch your driver. You do realize, do you not, that you need to leave immediately. The ride will be nearly one hundred miles, and your driver will need all of the daylight available to him if he is to get you there in two days."

The father and daughter exit the mansion and make their way to the awaiting carriage. A servant loads Peggy's luggage onto the carriage, and another assumes the driver's seat.

Edward Shippen assists his daughter up into the enclosed seating area of the coach. He stands on the running board, embraces Peggy, and pecks a soft kiss to her cheek. "Although I have never told the gentleman face-to-face, please communicate to him just what high regard I have always held for him."

"I will, Father, and thank you for helping me to be able to get to him at last."

"And thank you for teaching me your cryptography, my dear. Without those many ciphers, we could never have won the confidence of General Washington. I wonder just how long it will take old George to discover that he has been duped."

Peggy smiles.

The older and younger Shippen bid their farewells to each other, and the coach pulls out in a general northeasterly direction.

After an overnight stay at a friend's home on the Millstone River in New Jersey, Mrs. Arnold arrives at her destination—without her coach's approach being challenged by military sentries. Peggy never even has to show her pass.

As she nears her destination on Broadway Street, Peggy sees guards and an officer posted on foot. She concludes, *I think they have been awaiting my arrival.* Her carriage comes to a stop, and the officer assists Peggy down to the ground. While the guards unload her luggage, Peggy thinks, *I was correct.*

The two luggage carriers accompany Peggy as the officer leads her to the general's office.

The general stands and says, "Hello, hello."

Peggy rushes to the man, embraces him, and whispers, "John, I have missed you so much—and I have longed for you even more."

Peggy is sobbing.

John André, mirroring Peggy's embrace and her tears of joy, says, "I know. I know, my dearest Mrs. Arnold. Or should I say, my dearest widow Arnold?"

The couple's embrace leads to a kiss—a long and soft lovers' kiss. As the kiss ends, Peggy and John cling to each other.

"I love you, Peggy, but I feared that this war would never see us together again."

"Together we are, John. Thank God—and thanks to the invisible ink and ciphers we have shared for so long."

Their close embrace separates a few inches, and the couple holds hands.

John says, "And don't forget your father's role in Philadelphia as intermediary between me and Morristown."

"Yes, Father did fear for your safety and worried so about just how much risk you were taking in divulging so much inside information to your enemy."

"Sweet Peggy, with you as my prize, it would have been impossible to have risked too much. And besides, no amount of information learned by the upstart Colonials was going to save them from the mightiest army on the face of the earth. It was—and it is—just a matter of time."

"And, thank heavens, John, that our cryptic relationship can now become a transparent one."

"And you do envision, Dear Peggy, our relationship leading to matrimony, do you not?"

"Are you proposing to me, John?"

"Aye, my dearest, and only if you consent will I be able to believe that all of our labors—yours, mine, and your father's—in the name of our imaginary friend, the incomparable Agent 711, will have been worth it."

"Then my answer, John, is yes."

They embrace. His lips press hers until he suddenly stiffens his arms, pushes her shoulders inches away, and breaks out in laughter. John André almost giggles his words, saying, "Pardon me, dear, but it just occurred to me, Peggy, that we are quite correct about the fruits of our labors with our invisible spy. I remembered that extra little plum, you know, the bounty on Washington's life."

"But there was no assassination of the Colonials' commander in chief. My husband did not—"

"Peggy, we have duped more than one general, I'm happy to report. Over the weeks, I have managed to convince General Clinton that your husband really was planning to kill Washington."

"How were you able to?"

"Among other things, Peggy, I've shown Clinton portions of 711's final communiqué—the one mentioning the bounty to be transferred to Arnold's wife or other heirs in case of Benedict's demise."

"Clinton thinks that Agent 711 actually exists?"

"Not at all. The general believes that I personally offered Benedict the bounty through you—through you, Peggy—to your husband. So certain is Clinton that he has authorized me to convey to Arnold's widow his utmost gratitude for her role in all of this and to further convey to her half the bounty, which Clinton gladly would have paid her husband."

"You can't mean the ten thousand pounds sterling, can you, John?"

"Aye, the ten thousand pounds, now to be paid to the widow of the traitor, Benedict Arnold."

"Traitor?"

"My words, my darling, but do not be surprised. I dare say that in years to come, our frame-up of your husband will have guaranteed that the name Benedict Arnold—at least on this continent—shall become synonymous with treason. But enough about the dead, my love. As for the living, you and I should treat Clinton's ever-so-generous donation as a birthday present to you. Clinton's gift should make your birthday next year—that is, on July 11, 1781—your best one ever."

"John, you and I must celebrate and honor 7-11 for the rest of our lives."

EPILOGUE

In this novel, reader review of the pertinent espionage correspondence that was supplied to General George Washington would reveal the following chronologic sequence of events. First, there was the British plot to kidnap His Excellency. Second was Clinton's counterfeiting plan to deflate the Colonial currency. Third was the British plan to intercept French general Rochambeau's fleet at Newport, Rhode Island. Fourth was the enemy's plan to ambush George Washington at his conference with Rochambeau at New London, Connecticut.

These four intelligence communiqués, which steadily instilled in the general a deepening trust in and reliance upon Agent 711, all reached the commander in chief from Philadelphia.

General Washington's growing confidence in the veracity of his Philadelphia intelligence gatherer had laid the foundation for the fifth and final correspondence from that city. After the proven reliability of the earlier, invaluable messages from the Philadelphia agent, the credibility of any further communication beyond Spy 711's first four dispatches had been guaranteed.

The general's inevitable reaction to 711's missive number five was a conditioned response. Any communiqué from Agent 711 had become Washington's Pavlovian bell. The commander in chief could no more resist gushing at 711's signature than Pavlov's dogs could avoid salivating.

To Washington, the Philadelphian's message implicating Benedict Arnold in the assassination plot was prima facie evidence of Arnold's guilt; 711's word on it was sufficient to make the charge against Arnold a valid one in the eyes of the commander.

Interestingly, the first Philadelphia dispatch (warning of the Irishman kidnapper) that had been signed "711" had actually come from Peggy when she thought, *Perhaps the commander in chief might want to be my pen friend.*

Most of the intelligence that George Washington and Benedict Arnold thought was delivered by Agent 711 actually had been sent them from Agent 711's alter ego: Judge Edward Shippen.

Judge Shippen was being fed the intelligence by John André—from Franklin Muir, invisible ink letters, and André's encryption (in which the judge had been schooled by Peggy).

Edward Shippen also forwarded John André's ten thousand-pound bounty letter to Middleton, Connecticut, where Peggy had already planted the damning evidence of weapons and ammunition in Benedict's desk.

Judge Shippen deduced that the Colonial rebels were fighting for a losing cause, prompting him to join his daughter in their secret messaging with John André.

Arnold's failure to be promoted above the rank of major frustrated him, and it was a humiliation for Peggy. She could not continue to tolerate that indignity. While her husband was stagnating at a rank below colonel, John André had risen to the rank of general. John André was on the side of the war that she and her father favored anyway.

More than coincidentally, Benedict's continued failure to discover Agent 711's identity was a major impediment to being promoted by General Washington.

After her marriage, Peggy's lies, partial truths, and misleading statements included:

1. In response to Benedict's questioning her ability to decipher encrypted messages, she answered, "I and a former acquaintance of mine once undertook such sport just for amusement."
2. "And fortunate also that this new Agent 711—whoever he may be—is on our side."
3. In response to General Washington calling Agent 711 "hers," she said, "This Agent 711, well, he is not mine, I'm sure."
4. When Benedict noted that Judge Shippen had never used encryption, she said, "He has shown only little interest in my cryptography in the past, only a little curiosity."
5. When Benedict wondered why her father had not informed them about Agent 711's identity, she said, "I am uncertain. We surely have made enough requests of him."

Of course, Peggy and her father's choice of 711 as the code name for their fictitious spy was derived from Peggy Shippen's birthday, July 11.

Early on, Peggy refers to Colonel André as "Johnny." She is never inclined to call her husband "Benny."

APPENDIX A
Historical Figures' Quotations

A small portion of the novel's dialog has been borrowed from actual words from three of the book's historical characters: General Benedict Arnold, Major John André, and General George Washington.

- George Washington says, "Arnold! Whom can we trust now?" The general spoke those words to General Lafayette upon learning of Arnold's defection.
- Arnold actually penned a letter to his wife that said, "We are on the losing end of this war. You know that, I know that, thousands of Loyalists in this country know it."
- Arnold penned a letter to General Washington, saying, "If your Excellency thinks me criminal, for heaven's sake, let me be immediately tried and, if found guilty executed ... I ask only justice."
- Benedict (and Peggy) Arnold wrote an encrypted letter to Major John André that proclaims, "I am impressed that the mass of the people are heartily tired of the war."
- Benedict Arnold's February 8, 1779, letter to Peggy said, "I daily discover so much ingratitude among mankind that I almost blush at being of the same species, and could quit the stage without regret."
- At John André's own hanging, he said, "I pray you to bear me witness that I meet my fate like a brave man."

APPENDIX B
Fictional Characters Named in Honor of the Author's Family and the Author's Wife's Family

The author named the maid Laura in honor of his maternal grandmother's sister, Laura (Russell) Kyle. She and her husband, William, raised the author from childhood.

The author named John André's cousin, Franklin Muir, in honor of the author's paternal great-grandfather, John Franklin Metz and the author's wife's paternal great-grandmother, Margaret (Muir) Atkinson.

The author has named one fictional character, Lieutenant Scott Anderson, in honor of the author's maternal great-great-grandmother, Jean Scott (Anderson) Russell.

APPENDIX C

Historical Context and Disclaimers about the Book's Historical Figures

1. Chapter 1 mentions that Benedict Arnold had been paid no wages for months. Actually, Arnold had been paid no wages for years. Additionally, until 1779, Congress had not reimbursed Arnold for the expenditure of his own personal funds in the war effort.

2. Chapter 1 mentions Nathan Hale as being Benjamin Tallmadge's classmate and roommate at Yale College. Actually, Nathan Hale and Benjamin Tallmadge both graduated from Yale College in 1773.

3. Chapter 3 mentions five Culper Ring members: Agent 721, Benjamin Tallmadge (a.k.a. John Bolton), Agent 722, Abraham Woodhull (a.k.a. Samuel Culper), Agent 723, Robert Townsen (a.k.a. Samuel Culper Jr.), Agent 724, Austin Roe, and Agent 725, Caleb Brewster. Actually, other Culper Ring subagents or associates included Jonas Hawkins, Zachariah Hawkins, Hercules Mulligan, Selah Strong, Anna (Nancy) Smith Strong, Amos Underhill, and—probably, but not certainly—James Rivington, identified by Tallmadge as Agent 726.

4. Chapter 3 mentions petticoats hung on the clothesline of Abraham Woodhull's wife. Actually, Abraham Woodhull was instructed to watch for a black petticoat hanging on the clothesline of Anna Strong near Setauket Harbor. The black petticoat would indicate

that Caleb Brewster's boat had crossed Long Island Sound from Connecticut.

5. Chapter 3 mentions Caleb Brewster's boat. Actually, Brewster's vessel was a whaleboat. Caleb was from Setauket, which is where he took his whaleboat into Long Island Sound to harass the British.

6. Chapter 4 mentions the manor house at Mount Pleasant on the Schuylkill River. Actually, in 1779, Benedict Arnold bought Mount Pleasant for his bride, Peggy Shippen.

7. Chapter 4 mentions Washington's headquarters at the Ford Mansion at Morristown, New Jersey. Actually, on January 3, 1777, Washington established winter quarters at Morristown. Theodosia Ford, widow of Colonel Jacob Ford Jr. hosted General Washington at the Ford Mansion during the winter of 1779–80.

8. Chapter 6 mentions Benedict Arnold's marriage to Peggy Shippen. Actually, the Arnolds were married on April 8, 1779.

9. Chapter 6 mentions "ODD—GEORGE WASHINGTON" and "EVEN—JOHN ADAMS." Actually, the Culper spies did use the first three letters—GEO or JOH—as the keys in their cyphers.

10. Chapter 7 mentions Captain Alexander Hamilton. Actually, Hamilton became a lieutenant colonel as an aide to Washington, handling all of the general's correspondence, including intelligence.

11. Chapter 7 mentions the interrogation of Sergeant Thomas Hickey regarding the plot to kidnap George Washington. Actually, in 1776, Isaac Ketcham was arrested for his attempted counterfeiting of Colonial currency. In jail, Ketcham learned from his cellmate, Thomas Hickey (likewise jailed for counterfeiting), of Hickey's involvement in the conspiracy to kidnap George Washington. Ketcham gained his release by informing on Hickey. In addition, Ketcham implicated New York Governor William Tryon and New York City's Mayor David Matthews in that conspiracy.

12. Chapter 7 mentions Thomas Hickey's release to freedom to return to Ireland. Actually, Thomas Hickey, for his role in the conspiracy to kidnap General Washington, was tried, found guilty of high treason, and hanged—the first execution by the American army.

13. Chapter 7 mentions a message to General Washington that was signed by 711. Actually, in their spy messages, the Culper Ring used the number 711 to refer to the commander in chief.

14. Chapter 8 mentions Washington appointing Benedict Arnold as commander of the lifeguard. Actually, the lifeguard consisted of about 150 bodyguards. They also protected Washington's "baggage, papers, and other matters of great public import." Washington selected only men between five foot nine and five foot ten. He demanded "young, active, and well made" men who "possess the pride of appearing clean and soldierlike." Washington ordered the commanding officer of each of his regiments to nominate men for the guard who were "perfectly willing, and desirous, of being of this guard. They should be drill'd men."

15. Chapter 9 mentions the plan by Britain's general Clinton to make counterfeit Colonial currency. Actually, the English did flood the colonies with counterfeit bills, devaluing the American paper money—so severely that the Continental Congress had to retire the bills, ordering a $40 for $1 exchange in 1779. The whole $200,000,000 issued by the United States became worth zero dollars in 1781.

16. Chapter 12 mentions the relaying of a message from John André to Peggy Arnold. Actually, the first courier of messages between André and the Arnolds was Joseph Stansbury, a Tory Philadelphia merchant. The Arnolds and André used codes written in invisible ink, hidden between the lines in seemingly innocent correspondence ostensibly between Peggy and her friends.

17. Chapter 12 mentions General Henry Clinton's desire to set a land trap for the French fleet at Newport, Rhode Island. Actually, before Clinton could send his soldiers to Newport, Washington allowed a false battle plan to fall into British hands. The plan outlined a fictitious attack on New York City, which was designed to convince General Clinton to keep his troops in that city and not send them to Rhode Island. Washington also moved some troops toward New York in a feint to gather Clinton's attention. The result was that Clinton stayed home and did not lay an ambush for the French

119

general Rochambeau in Rhode Island. Thus, the French fleet successfully landed in Newport.

18. Chapter 14 mentions Washington's twenty-eight Morristown regiments of about 5,600 men in each, totaling about 22,400 men. Actually, during the winter of 1776–7, Washington's numbers at Morristown shrunk to about one thousand. Spring recruits raised his corps to about nine thousand. At Morristown, after the harsh winter of 1779–80, two of Washington's regiments conducted an armed march through the camp, demanding payment of overdue salary. Pennsylvania troops put down the mutiny, and two of the protest leaders were hanged.

19. Chapter 14 mentions a fake battle plan that mimicked Britain's 1776 attack on Fort Washington. Actually, in the real 1776 battle against the Colonialists, some British and/or Hessian troops did approach Fort Washington via King's Bridge, Flatbush Road, and Shoemaker's Bridge.

20. Chapter 14 mentions a false battle plan for an attack upon New York. Actually, near the end of the war in 1781, Washington did try to make Clinton think he was planning to attack him by building big army camps and big brick ovens visible from New York. In addition, Washington allowed signed, false papers describing his plans for an attack on New York to fall into the hands of the British. Leaving only a small rear guard behind, Washington and French general Rochambeau—instead of invading New York—led their troops to Yorktown to confront Cornwallis. This led to the British surrender.

21. Chapter 16 mentions Peggy Arnold's birthday as July 11. Actually, Peggy Shippen was born on June 11, 1760.

22. Chapter 18 mentions Washington's changing of his conference site with General Rochambeau. Actually, in February 1781, a New York tailor, Hercules Mulligan, warned General Washington about a plot to kidnap the commander in chief. Mulligan advised Washington that the British, at Lebanon, Connecticut, were laying a three hundred-man cavalry trap for General Washington. Therefore, the commander changed his route to Newport, Rhode Island, to a safer, more inland one to confer with Rochambeau.

23. Chapter 20 mentions Washington's discovery of Benedict Arnold's plan to assassinate the commander in chief. Actually, when Washington first learned of Arnold's plan to turn over West Point to the enemy, Washington was heard to exclaim to General Lafayette, "Arnold has betrayed me! Whom can we trust now?"

24. Chapter 21 mentions Benedict Arnold's saying, "If your Excellency thinks me criminal, for heaven's sake, let me be immediately tried and, if found guilty executed ... I ask only justice." Actually, Arnold wrote those exact words to Washington in 1779, urging the commander in chief to expedite Arnold's court-martial. At that time, Benedict had been accused of allegedly having used his position as military commander of Philadelphia to make improper financial gains. Arnold's 1779 letter to Washington concluded with, "Having made every sacrifice of fortune and blood, and become a cripple in the service of my country, I little expected to meet the ungrateful returns I have received from my countrymen ... Delay in the present case is worse than death." In Arnold's case, the court issued a formal reprimand.

25. Chapter 21 mentions the court-martial of Benedict Arnold. Actually, the historic Benedict Arnold was not tried for his involvement in the West Point conspiracy because Arnold fled to the safety of the British Army and escaped any punishment at all by the Colonial Army. Benedict and Peggy Arnold both were received by the British and lived most of the rest of their lives in England. In 1780, John André was captured and punished. André was captured behind American lines, using the alias John Anderson and having in his possession papers implicating Arnold in Benedict's plan to turn over West Point to the British. André's captors were John Paulding, David Williams, and Isaac Van Wart, each later to be given a US pension of $200 a year and a silver medal. André was tried as a spy, convicted, and hanged by the Continental Army.

26. Chapter 21 mentions Generals Stirling, St. Clair, Lafayette, Howe, Steuben, Parsons, Clinton, Knox, Glover, Paterson, Hand, Huntington, and Stark in the court martial of Benedict Arnold. Actually, those generals formed the panel of judges in the trial of John André.

27. Chapter 22 mentions Benedict Arnold saying, "I am impressed that the mass of the people are heartily tired of the war" and "I daily discover so much ingratitude among mankind that I almost blush to be of the same species." Actually, in a July 12, 1780, coded message to John André, Benedict Arnold wrote, "I am impressed that the mass of the people are heartily tired of the war." Additionally, Benedict Arnold wrote a letter to Peggy on February 8, 1779, that said, "My dearest life … I daily discover so much baseness and ingratitude among mankind that I almost blush at being of the same species, and could quit the stage without regret."

28. Chapter 22 contains Benedict Arnold's request for execution by firing squad rather than by hanging. Actually, John André appealed to George Washington to substitute an execution by firing squad for execution by hanging. Washington, however, abiding by the rules of war involving espionage, denied André's request. André was hanged as a spy at Tappan, New York, on October 2, 1780. British general Henry Clinton tried in vain to save André from execution but refused Washington's proposal to swap André for Arnold. André's death was lamented by many American officers. Alexander Hamilton described André's execution: "Never perhaps did any man suffer death with more justice, or deserve it less."

29. Chapter 23 mentions Benedict Arnold's request to forgo blindfolding and be allowed to place the rope around his neck himself. Actually John André refused the blindfold and voluntarily put his neck into the noose.

30. Chapter 23 mentions Benedict Arnold's last words on the gallows: "I pray you to bear me witness that I meet my fate like a brave man." Actually, those were John André's last words.

APPENDIX D
The Spies

Robert Townsend

When Robert Townsend joined the spy ring, the Culper leader, Benjamin Tallmadge—because Tallmadge's younger brother was named Samuel—bestowed upon Robert the moniker of Samuel Culper Jr., the only name by which Washington ever knew Townsend.

Townsend and James Rivington (possibly a Culper affiliate) were partners in a New York City coffeehouse, where Townsend (and Rivington) would mingle with high-ranking British officers (including John André), extracting valuable intelligence from the unsuspecting redcoats.

Sarah Townsend often provided her brother with information from her conversations with British officers staying at the Townsend home.

Robert portrayed himself so well as a Loyalist that he was allowed to write articles for the King's newspaper (edited by James Rivington). Robert would publicize the exploits of British officers he knew. The British soldiers whose names and military activities were written about by Townsend seemed to be promoted in rank more quickly by the British army, so they were eager to share their stories with Townsend.

Typically, Townsend would receive General Washington's requests for information from the Culpers' land courier, Austin Roe, to whom Townsend would in turn deliver data to be delivered back to General Washington.

Austin Roe

Roe was often called the Paul Revere of the spy network. He was the Culper Ring's primary land courier. Because Roe was a tavern owner in Setauket, the British had grown accustomed to his traveling between New York City and his hometown on business supply runs. In the city, Roe would deliver information or requests that had come from General Washington by way of Setauket's Abraham Woodhull to Robert Townsend, a coffeehouse proprietor. Townsend would pass on his intelligence data (usually in invisible ink) to Roe. Riding the fifty-five miles back to Setauket, Roe would deliver the paper to Abraham Woodhull's farm (but not directly to Woodhull). Instead, Roe would deposit whatever message he had been carrying into a box and bury the box at a designated spot in Woodhull's field.

Abraham Woodhull

General Washington chose Woodhull's alias to be Samuel Culper because the initials reversed those of Washington's aide, General Charles Scott. At seventeen, Washington had been a surveyor in Virginia's Culpeper County. Evidently, Washington amused himself by pronouncing "Culpeper" as "Culper."

Early in his spying career, Woodhull would frequently visit his sister, Mary, at the Underbill Boardinghouse on Queen Street in New York City. There, Woodhull would overhear talkative redcoats discussing supplies, shipping, and troop movements. In 1779, fearing for his safety after too frequently having been stopped by British military, Woodhull found a replacement in Robert Townsend, who insisted that Woodhull pledge never to reveal Townsend's identity. It appears that Woodhull did inform Ben Tallmadge. After Townsend replaced Woodhull, Abraham returned to his farm life in Setauket.

In Setauket, when Austin Roe would plant his boxed intelligence information in Woodhull's field, Abraham would retrieve the report and use a telescope to check the neighboring clothesline of Anna Smith Strong. If Anna had hung a black petticoat out to dry, that was Woodhull's signal that Caleb Brewster's boat had arrived in town. Additionally, the number of white handkerchiefs on the line would indicate in which of Setauket's six coves Brewster was waiting. Woodhull would ride to the designated inlet to relay Roe's message to Brewster.

Caleb Brewster

Brewster was the Culpers' primary courier by sailing vessel. A lifelong friend of Benjamin Tallmadge, the Colonial Army captain would take his whale-boat onto Long Island Sound to harass the enemy. Bold and confident, Brewster never used his 725 code name, always signing his intelligence missives with his full name.

Part of Brewster's sailing route was from Fairfield, Connecticut, across Long Island Sound, carrying secret dispatches from Washington or Tallmadge to Abraham Woodhull on Long Island. The messages might be disguised as shopping lists or some other ostensibly innocuous correspondences.

The other part of Brewster's route found him sailing from Long Island to Fairfield. That trip from Setauket to Connecticut was Brewster's part in the relay of intelligence that had been transferred from New York's Robert Townsend to Austin Roe, from Roe to Abraham Woodhull, from Woodhull to Brewster, soon from Brewster to Tallmadge, and finally from Tallmadge to General Washington.

Major Benjamin Tallmadge

In the summer of 1778, Washington assigned Major Benjamin Tallmadge to create a network of civilian spies in New York City. Having been born on Long Island, and still having ties to the local community, Tallmadge decided to make Setauket the hub of Culper Ring. Tallmadge recruited for his first agents two of his friends (Abraham Woodhull and Robert Townsend) and two other Long Islanders (Caleb Brewster and Austin Roe).

When John André was captured behind American lines, his American captors immediately messaged their commander at West Point, Benedict Arnold, and sent Arnold the incriminating documents found with André. Benjamin Tallmadge, suspecting that André was a spy and that Benedict Arnold was his accomplice, tried—but failed—to convince his superiors to refrain from notifying Arnold. Tallmadge did, however, manage to gain custody of André until the British officer's execution.

Anna Strong

Also known as Nancy, she lived in Setauket—within sight of Abraham Woodhull's farm. On one of Woodhull's trips to New York City, Anna posed as his wife because couples drew less suspicion than a lone man traveling to or from the city.

Anna Strong would signal Woodhull with a black petticoat on her clothesline to notify him that Caleb Brewster's boat had made it to across the sound. Additionally, the number of white handkerchiefs on the line signified to Woodhull in which inlet he could find Brewster hiding.

James Rivington

In New York, Rivington was the king's official printer. In his Tory newspaper, the *Royal Gazette*, Rivington exaggerated the losses of the Americans while giving short shrift to British failures. His ostensible dedication—or perhaps actual dedication—to the king made Rivington privy to British military information. Historians debate whether Rivington was or was not one of Washington's spies.

Evidence tending to affirm Rivington's espionage endeavors for the Colonials includes the fact that Robert Townsend was a contributing journalist at the *Royal Gazette* and that James also was co-owner of the New York coffeehouse.

Additional positive evidence that Rivington was a spy for the Colonials is found in five documents:

1. Benjamin Tallmadge's code dictionary listed Rivington as Agent 726.
2. A 1781 letter to George Washington from the director of the Board of War, Judge Richard Peters, describes Rivington's printing office as a place "where there is a Person ready to furnish any important Papers as Intelligence." Although by saying "person," Peters might have meant Robert Townsend.

126

3. William Hooper wrote to James Iredell that, "Rivington has been very useful to Gen. Washington by furnishing him with intelligence."
4. The memoirs of Allen McLane, one of Washington's informants, stated, "I ... was imployed by the board of war to repair to Long Island to watch the motion of the British fleet and if possible obtain their Signals which I did threw the assistance of the noteed Rivington."
5. Among Allen McLane's papers, a document revealed that Allen McLane "was stationed by the Board of War near Sandyhook to correspond with R of New York received the Signals for the British fleet out of New York delivered them to Count De Grass acted occasionally on the Shore and with the French fleet after Cornwallis had surrendered."

Agent 355

Rumor prevailed that there was a female—Agent 355—associated with the Culper Ring. In Tallmadge's notebook, 355 perhaps stood for only a lady in general, not any specific lady. Other references in Culper code to gender included: 371 (man), 237 (gentleman), and 701 (woman).

One interpretation of the Culper code numbers is that 701 might be a female servant, but 355 might be a woman from a rich, prominent family.

A mention of 355 in one of Tallmadge's messages references New York (the city labeled 727 in Culper code): "I intend to visit 727 before long and think by the assistance of a 355 of my acquaintance, shall be able to outwit them all." The indefinite article "a" preceding the "355" might mean that Tallmadge is saying more generally "some lady" and not necessarily substituting 355 for the name of one specific female Culper Ring spy.

The possible distinction between the Culpers' 701 and 355 has led some historians to speculate about the existence of an actual, individual woman—a Loyalist woman from New York society.

The writings of another Culper spy, Abraham Woodhull, imply that 355 was one distinct person. She was a valuable informant: "one who hath been ever serviceable to this correspondence."

Supposedly, Benedict Arnold believed that Agent 355 existed prior to his defection to the British army. Thereupon, he initiated a roundup of all New Yorkers whom he suspected of espionage for the Colonials. It is speculated that one among those arrested—per Arnold's instructions—perhaps was Agent 355, rumored to have been Robert Townsend's lover. It is further speculated that the pregnant Agent 355 was sentenced to the ill-famed British prison ship HMS *Jersey* in New York Harbor. She allegedly delivered a son whom it is further alleged that she named Robert Townsend Jr. before she died amid the grossly unsanitary conditions of the ship.

THE CULPER RING'S SPY MESSAGING ROUTE

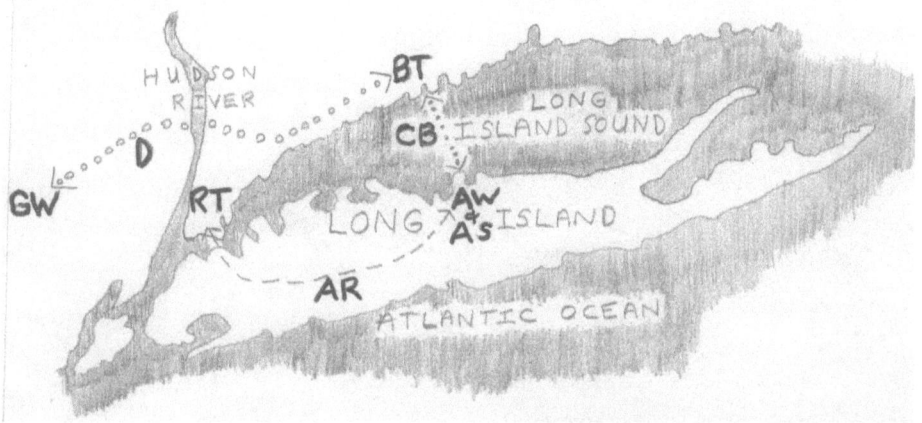

The Culper Ring's Spy Messaging Route
GW = George Washington at Morristown, New Jersey
D = Dragoon rider's path between Morristown and Fairfield
BT = Benjamin Tallmadge at Fairfield, Connecticut
CB = Caleb Brewster's boat route between Fairfield and Setauket
AW & AS = Abraham Woodhull and Anna Strong at Setauket
AR = Austin Roe's overland route between Setauket and New York City
RT = Robert Townsend's coffeehouse in New York City

APPENDIX E

Cryptography—Invisible Ink, Codes, and Ciphers

The Culpers communicated among themselves as Benedict and Peggy Arnold communicated with John Andre—by using invisible ink, codes, and ciphers.

Invisible Ink

1. Despite the advantages of invisible ink, it had its shortcomings. Because the ink was made of juices from natural sources such as vinegar, urine, potatoes, oranges, milk, limes, leeks, and cabbage, it was easy to expose the dried ink message simply by applying heat—as easy for foe, unfortunately, as it was for friend. According to the historian Alexander Rose, "The very simplicity of the revelatory process tended to outweigh the advantages bestowed by invisibility."
2. John Adams and Ben Franklin used invisible ink.
3. Before the Revolutionary War, a physician, Sir James Jay, and his brother, John Jay (future chief justice of the US Supreme Court) developed a more secure invisible ink chemistry. The "white ink" and "sympathetic stain" did not rely on heat. Instead, the writer of the correspondence used one chemical and the receiver used a second ("sympathetic") chemical to develop it.
4. General Washington directed his spies to use Jay's invisible ink. Washington wrote to his spymaster, Benjamin Tallmadge: "I send

twenty guineas and two fials containing the stain and counterpart of the stain for C___ Jr. which I wish may be got to him with as much safety and dispatch as will conveniently admit of."

5. James Jay recommended that the invisible ink message be hidden between the lines of an otherwise innocent-appearing letter. The Culpers sometimes hid their white ink words among the lines of a "shopping list." Robert Townsend used blank paper, hiding the stained page in a prearranged, specific layer inside a ream of paper.

Codes

1. A code does not change individual letters, but it does change whole words or whole phrases.

2. A code changes entire words or phrases into a group of numbers, into other words or phrases, or into symbols based on a list or a book.

3. A book code (sometimes called a "dictionary code") requires that the code sender and recipient both possess the same book, for instance, a dictionary or the Bible. A sender's encoded word might be symbolized as 155.16.3 and could be decoded by using the recipient's book—the coded word being the third word on line 16 of page 155.

4. In July 1779, Benjamin Tallmadge devised a book code using the 1771 *New Latin and English Dictionary*, which he issued to the Culpers and General Washington.

5. John Andre suggested to Benedict Arnold that they use a book code based upon either *Blackstone's Commentaries on the Laws of England* or Nathan Bailey's *Universal Etymological Dictionary*.

6. Benjamin Tallmadge used a numerical substitution code. Tallmadge substituted the numbers 1 through 763 for several hundred dictionary words and several dozen proper nouns. For example, New York was replaced by #727, #712 represented General George Clinton, George Washington was identified as #711, #192 meant "fort," and #38 stood for "attack."

Ciphers

1. A cipher rearranges individual letters or changes individual letters into numbers, symbols, or other letters by utilizing a prearranged setting known as a key.
2. John Adams and Ben Franklin used ciphers.
3. James Lovell, a member of the Continental Congress's Committee of Foreign Affairs, deciphered most or all of the British coded messages intercepted by the Americans.

Lovell also developed a cipher system of his own that employed a secret key word—a word agreed upon by the sender and the recipient of the cipher. Furthermore, whatever the agreed upon key word would be, the cipher would utilize only the first three letters of that word. For example, if the key word for the cipher was "George Washington," then only the G, E, and O would be used in the ciphering and deciphering.

Lovell's system required the use of a written chart or table consisting of three columns of letters in alphabetic order (no column would begin with the letter A). In any column, whichever line that the Z was on would be followed beneath the Z by the letter A on the next line down, with B on the next row under that, followed by all of the remaining letters of the alphabet, in order, down the page.

From the keyword *George Washington*, Lovell would use the first three letters. He would write the G at the top of the left column, E at the top of the middle column, and O at the top of the right column.

In order to understand Lovell's cipher chart, one needs to know (simplified here for illustration) that the letters in the chart's left column are useful in ciphering or deciphering only the first letter of a word, the letters in the middle column are useful in ciphering or deciphering only the second letter of a word, and the letters in the right column are useful in ciphering or deciphering only the third letter of a word.

The G at the top of the left column would become the initial letter of that column's vertical, alphabetic list of letters and would continue beneath the G with H on the next line down, then I below that, followed by J down the column to Z.

Likewise, the E at the top of the middle column would become the initial

133

letter of that column's vertical, alphabetic list of letters and would continue beneath the E with F on the next line, then G below that, followed by H down the column to Z.

Similarly, the O at the top of the right column would become the initial letter of that column's vertical, alphabetic list of letters that would continue beneath the O with P on the next line, then Q below that, followed by R down the column to Z.

Note that Lovell's chart (again, simplified here for illustration) would contain only twenty-six numbered lines, a row for each of the twenty-six letters of the alphabet. In Lovell's ciphering, the chart's numbers substitute for the letters of a word. Which letter the number stands for in a ciphered word depends upon whether that letter is the first letter of the word, the second letter of the word, the third letter of the word, etc.

Lovell's chart now becomes slightly more complex. Lovell always added one extra row to the twenty-six rows in his chart. In a twenty-seventh row, he added a twenty-seventh symbol to the twenty-six alphabetic letters. Just below the Z in each column's alphabet list, he added the ampersand symbol (&), which became the twenty-seventh symbol in that column. Thus in each column the & was always beneath the Z and above the A, allowing the A to restart the sequence down the vertical list.

Additionally, whatever letter was found on the chart column's bottom line—let's say, a D on the twenty-seventh line of the middle column—then the alphabet resumed with the letter E at the top of that same column.

The following is the way a Lovell ciphering chart would look, using just the first three letters (G, E, O) of George Washington:

A JAMES LOVELL CIPHERING CHART

	Coded Word's 1st Letter And 4th Letter	Coded Word's 2nd Letter And 5th Letter	Coded Word's 3rd Letter And 6th Letter
Key's 1st 3 letters:	G	E	O
1	G	E	O
2	H	F	P
3	I	G	Q
4	J	H	R
5	K	I	S
6	L	J	T
7	M	K	U
8	N	L	V
9	O	M	W
10	P	N	X
11	Q	O	Y
12	R	P	Z
13	S	Q	&
14	T	R	A
15	U	S	B
16	V	T	C
17	W	U	D
18	X	V	E
19	Y	W	F
20	Z	X	G
21	&	Y	H
22	A	Z	I
23	B	&	J
24	C	A	K
25	D	B	L
26	E	C	M
27	F	D	N

135

By using the above chart, one could write the cipher for JOHN as 4, 11, 21, 8.

Because J is the first letter in JOHN, and because J is found on line 4 in the chart's left (1st letter, G) column, the 4 stands for the first letter (J).

Because O is the second letter in JOHN, and because O is found on line 11 in the chart's middle (second letter, E) column, the 11 stands for the second letter (O).

Because H is the third letter in JOHN, and because H is found on line 21 in the chart's right (third letter, O) column, the 21 stands for the third letter (H).

Because N is the fourth letter in JOHN, and because N is found on line 8 in the chart's G (fourth letter—using the left column again) column, the 8 stands for the fourth letter (N).

If the ciphered word needed a fifth letter, it would be found in the chart's E (middle, fifth letter) column.

If the ciphered word needed a sixth letter, it would be found in the chart's O (right, sixth letter) column.

Any additional letters beyond a sixth letter in the ciphered word can be found in the chart's G column for a seventh letter, in the E column for an eighth letter, in the O column for a ninth letter, etc.

Hiding Places

1. Dead drop: A dead drop was a designated place, e.g. inside a hollow root of a tree or a hole in the ground, where the deliverer of the message would hide his paper to be picked up later by the recipient. Thus, the delay from the planting of the note by one Culper agent and receiving of the message by the second operative guaranteed that even if the dead drop location were to be discovered by the enemy, only one of the spies, at the most, could be captured while visiting that site.

2. Inside common, everyday containers: Some whole sheets containing an invisible ink message were inserted into a designated depth inside a ream of apparently blank papers. Flattened or folded messages were slipped inside a double-sided canteen, and long, narrow, messages were rolled on a sheet of paper and inserted into a large, hollow quill feather.

3. Inside a swallowed silver ball: Captured British spy Daniel Taylor swallowed a silver ball containing a hidden message. American Dr. Moses Higby gave Taylor an emetic that induced vomiting. Taylor quickly grabbed the silver ball from his vomit and swallowed the ball again. Taylor refused to take another dose of the emetic until American general George Clinton threatened to hang him and excise the silver ball from his innards. Taylor reconsidered and took the emetic. The ball was regurgitated once more and broken open, revealing a note written by British general Henry Clinton.

4. Masks: A long, innocent-looking correspondence could have its contained, shorter, secret spy message revealed by covering the long message with a sheet of paper, from which a portion had been cut out to form some geometric or other shape. The paper cover sheet would shield most of the communiqué with only the smaller, pertinent message showing itself within the boundaries of the cut-out space. The Culper Ring used a cover sheet that had the shape of an hourglass cut from its center. With the cover sheet masking everything above, below, left of, and right of the hourglass shape, the Culper message would be revealed.

In the following example, the top paragraph represents an ostensibly innocent correspondence about coats of arms, talcum powder, and clay pot firing. The middle shape represents the mask, which when placed upon the paragraph reveals the spy message about arms, gunpowder, and flints for firing weapons.

We shall be sending in next shipment your often requested 2 or 3 coats of arms for the family. You can return empty crates by cart on the 12th or 13th to their place of origin. We need also talcum powder for our friends. We also will need a few more of stone flints and lbs of clay for pot & for firing.

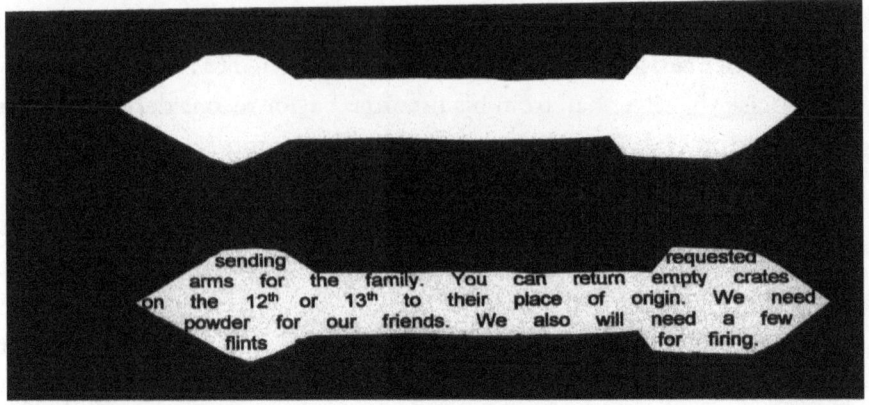

Mask Similar to That Used by the Culper Ring

APPENDIX F

Peggy and Benedict Arnold Communicate with John André

The following is a reproduction of what originally was a handwritten, coded communication, dated 7/12/1780, by Benedict and Peggy Arnold to Colonel John André.

120.9.7, W------- 105.9.5's on the .22.9.14.---- / of 163.8.19 F----- 172.8.7s to 56.9.8 |30.000| 172.8.70 to 11.94. in / 62.8.20. If 179.8.25, 84.8.9'd, 177.9.28. N---- is 111.9.27.'d on / 23.8.10. the 111.9.13, 180.9.19 if his 180.8.21 an .179.8.25., 255.8.17. for / that, 180.9.19, 44.8.9—a—is the 234.8.14 of 189.8.17. I --- / 44.8.9, 145.8.17, 294.9.12, in 266.8.17 as well as, 103.8.11, 184.9.15.---- / 80.4.20. ---- I149.8.7, 10.8.22'd the 57.9.71 at 288.9.9, 198.9.26, as, a / 100.4.18 in 189.8.19—I can 221.8.6 the 173.8.19, 102.8.26, 236.8.21's--- / and 289.8.17 will be in 175.9.7, 87.8.7--- the 166.8.11, of the .191.9.16 / are .129.19.21 'of --- 266.9.14 of the .286.8.20, and 291.8.27 to be an ---163.9.4 / 115.8.16 -'a .114.8.25ing --- 263.9.14. are 207.8.17ed, 125.8.15, 103.8.60--- / from this 294.8.50, 104.9.26—If 84.8.9ed—294.9.12, 129.8.7. only / to 193.8.3 and the 64.9.5, 290.9.20, 245.8.3 be at an, 99.8.14 . / the .204.8.2,

253.8.7s are 159.8.10 the 187.8.11 of a 94.9.9ing / 164.8.24, 279.8.16, but of a .238.8.25, 93.9.28.

The following is the decoding of the above Arnolds' note done by Jonathan Odell, André's assistant. The decoded message reveals Benedict Arnold's early negotiations regarding his planned surrender of West Point to the British.

General W[ashington]—expects on the arrival of the F[rench]—Troops to collect / 30,000 Troops to act in conjunction; if not disappointed, N[ew]. York is fixed / on as the first Object, if his numbers are not sufficient for that Object, / Can-a- is the second; of which I can inform you in time, as well as of / every other design. I have accepted the command at W[est]. P[oint]. As a Post in which / I can render the most essential Services, and which will be in my disposal. / The mass of the People are heartily tired of the War, and wish to be on / their former footing - They are promised great events from this / year's exertion—If - disappointed - you have only to persevere / and the contest will soon be at an end. The present Struggles are / like the pangs of a dying man, violent but of a short duration –

APPENDIX G
Commentary

The following commentary about some of the historical figures in *If This Be Treason* was issued by the historical figures' contemporaries or by biographers.

John André

Biographer Henry Cabot Lodge wrote, "André was a trafficker in bribes and treachery, and however we may pity his fate, his name has no proper place in the great temple at Westminster, where all English-speaking people bow with reverence, and only a most perverted sentimentality could conceive that it was fitting to erect a monument to his memory in this country."

Leader of the Culper Spy Ring, Major Benjamin Tallmadge wrote of his admiration for André, "From the time of his [André's] being brought back to our head-quarters to the day of his execution, I became so deeply attached to Major Andre, that I can remember no instance where my affections were so fully absorbed in any man."

Tallmadge further opined, "Had he [André] been tried by a Court of ladies, he is so genteel, handsome, polite a young gentleman, that I am confident they would have acquitted him."

America's major general William Heath (Arnold's successor as West Point's commander), said, "He who consents to become a spy, when he sets out, has by allusion a halter put round his neck, and that … if he be taken, the other end of the halter is speedily made fast to a gallows."

George Washington said, "I am mistaken if at this time Arnold is undergoing the torment of a mental hell. He wants feeling. From some traits of his character which have lately come to my knowledge, he seems to have been so hackneyed in villainy, and so lost to all sense of honor and shame, that, while his faculties will enable him to continue his sordid pursuits, there will be no time for remorse."

History.org describes Arnold as "probably the best field commander on either side in the Revolution. His invasion of Canada, compared by contemporaries to Hannibal's crossing the Alps, had nearly succeeded in making that province the fourteenth state. Skillful and bold, he had won the Battle of Saratoga, reversing the Americans' losing streak and securing French assistance for Ambassador Benjamin Franklin. He also sustained a severe leg wound that, for a time, sidelined him to garrison duty, and gave him more time to brood on the under-appreciation of his brilliance."

Americanheritage.com says, "No blaring trumpets had welcomed the fleeing traitor to Great Britain's American stronghold. Not that he had cause to complain. Sir Henry Clinton and his generals punctiliously bestowed on him all the consideration due a competent military man who in their opinion, of course, was merely a rebel who had seen the light and had returned to his proper allegiance. Treason had deprived Arnold of his American rank of major general; but Sir Henry assigned to him the highest British military rating ever given an American colonial, that of colonel of a regiment, with the rank of brigadier general of provincials and the authority to raise a Loyalist legion.

"Below the upper echelons at headquarters, however, Arnold's presence was resented. A local newspaper noted that the 'General … is a very unpopular character in the British army, nor can all the patronage he meets with from the commander-in-chief procure him respectability'

"Sir Henry Clinton … was aware that beyond the ramparts of New York the traitor would be the object of fierce enemy action. Even within the city Arnold was unsafe: an elaborate scheme by the Americans to kidnap him from the garden of his home one evening came within a hairbreadth of succeeding. Only twice did Sir Henry permit the traitor to take to the field against his countrymen. Both were diversionary forays of no strategic importance."

More from history.org (paraphrased here): Later in his life, as a privateer in 1795, Arnold was captured by the French and imprisoned as a spy. To the French, Benedict protested that he was an American citizen, choosing the alias, John Anderson—the same alias earlier used by John André when the Americans captured him. After Arnold's death in 1801, British media described the deceased merely as "a person much noticed during the American War."

Peggy (Shippen) Arnold

Answers.com reports, "She [Peggy Shippen] had been a great favorite of the British officers during the nine months they had held Philadelphia—one described her as 'most drenchingly lovely.'" Answers.com adds: "How much of his [Arnold's] treason was due to the influence of his highly manipulative, young, spoiled lovely wife is a matter of conjecture."

Scandalouswoman.blogspot.com writes, "After her death, a biographer of Aaron Burr first made the claim that Peggy had either manipulated or convinced Arnold to change sides ... The information came from Burr's wife, Theodosia Prevost, who had been a good friend of Peggy's. Peggy had stayed with Prevost in what is now Paramus, NJ, en route to Philadelphia from West Point. Apparently Peggy couldn't take the lying anymore and confessed everything to Theodosia, telling her that 'through unceasing perseverance, she had ultimately brought the general into an arrangement to surrender West Point.' When the biography was published, the Shippen family disputed this version of events. They claim that Burr made up these allegations because Peggy had spurned his advances made on the way to Philadelphia. However, papers were later found that showed that Peggy was paid £350 for handling secret dispatches."

Americanheritage.com chimes in: "Only hearsay supports the story of her confession to an acquaintance that it was she who had persuaded her husband to betray his country, but such an action would have been in keeping with her character and background ... Peggy was an ardent Tory, and she was ambitious. She realized that if the general aided the British substantially, he would be well rewarded. A grateful king might even give him a title.

Then someday, after years of gracious living in England, she could return to Philadelphia to be deferred to by her friends as 'Lady Arnold.'

"It was the collapse of these dreams that sent her into apparent hysterics on September 25, 1780, when word reached West Point that the treason conspiracy had been discovered, and her frantic husband made his last-minute escape, leaving Peggy and her six-month-old son to the kind mercies of George Washington and his aides. Washington gave her a choice. She could join her husband in British-held New York or her family in Philadelphia. She chose Philadelphia, but the local authorities refused to let her stay. By November she and her baby were in New York, living with Arnold in a fine house he had leased next door to British headquarters at Broadway and Wall Street."

Amazon.com's review of *Treacherous Beauty*, the biography of Peggy Shippen, perhaps sums up the consensus opinion about the Arnold-Arnold-André trio: "When you are done reading you won't like Benedict Arnold at all and may not have the sympathy you once had for Major André. The jury is still out on Peggy Shippen. It is probably safe to say that all three got what they deserved in the end."